An Interview With Jesus Christ

Joseph Head

ISBN-13: 978-1515083382

ISBN-10: 1515083381

Table of Contents

PART ONE – THE INTERVIEW

DAY ONE

Greg Miller is my name. I spend my days working for a national news magazine that is, unfortunately, now in decline. The magazine is being kept afloat by its owners to satisfy their loyal subscribers, but it's really on the way out. I got the job of "reporter" through the intervention of an uncle who formerly served as one of their editors. The office itself is just a satellite in our city with few employees and not much to do.

I was surprised, therefore, to receive an email stating that I was to expect a visitor by the name of Mr. Jesus Christ, and I was to conduct an interview with him that might be considered for a lead story in one of our upcoming issues. Included in the email was a short list of talking points intended to facilitate the process.

To say that I am a novice at this is quite an understatement. This is, in fact, the first interview I have ever conducted, and why I was selected is anyone's guess. I suppose the owners wanted to distance themselves from the subject matter while at the same time hoping for some kind of a sensational story.

I really just wanted to get it over with and move onto more important matters.

When I walked into my office that first day I was surprised to find him already sitting there. I was so self absorbed and nervous that I hardly registered any first impressions. But in retrospect I beheld a man in his late 30s to early 40s, neatly dressed, of average height. His face was magnificent, very masculine, with brilliant grey eyes and a large, open countenance. He looked as though he had been in a few fistfights in his younger days, but that only added to his overall good looks. Although he appeared to be supremely self-confident, there was not a trace of arrogance or condescension in his manner. It was quite the opposite. He seemed to be mostly interested in what *I* had to say.

I might add that the room seemed unusually quiet. The phone never rang. There were no interruptions. There was no chatter in the hallway, no radio playing in the distance. Even the traffic on the street was subdued. No honking horns, no screeching brakes. It was almost as if the entire city, including the buildings and streets, were standing in hushed awe at the presence of this most exalted visitor.

At the time, as I said, I was quite oblivious to any of this.

I introduced myself as soon as I entered, and he stood up to shake my outstretched hand. Then, resuming his seat, he said, "I meet a lot of people, and when I tell a joke they want to know why I'm not serious, and when I'm serious they complain that I never crack a smile! Some of these people are a real pain in the buttocks!" Then he winked at me and asked, "What's on your mind today?"

"Well, I do have some questions…"

"Right. Questions…" There was something in his demeanor. I could see that he was eager to begin, but I thought I detected just the faintest hint of weariness. Looking at me as if he were trying to size me up, he said, "Listen, what do you say we skip the formalities? We could pop open a nice bottle of Muscadet and order a platter of fresh oysters!"

For God's sake, it's 9 o'clock in the morning! What is this guy thinking?

"Um, I'll call the receptionist…"

He put up his hand. "That's okay, Greg. Never mind. What was I thinking? Come on, let's do this. Ask me some of your questions."

"Okay…" I checked my notes and took a deep breath. "Well, I understand, or shall I say I've heard, that you are running for, what is it? President of the World?"

"That's right. I'm running for President of the World."

"Really? I guess I didn't realize there was such a position as 'President of the World' that was needing to be filled."

"The position is open." he replied. "I would be the first person to hold that office, and once I'm elected I intend to keep the job pretty much forever."

Are you for real? Are you completely insane? I am beginning to understand why I was chosen to conduct this interview. The man is clearly delusional. I collect my wits and proceed cautiously…

"So, then, Mr. Christ. Let's back up for a minute, can we? Word on the street is that you claim to be God. Do you claim to be God? Or to put it more bluntly, are you God Almighty?"

"Yes, I am." Said with a perfectly straight face.

I paused long enough to think to myself, *"This is pure nonsense."* To him I said, "With all due respect, sir, why on earth would God want to be elected 'President of the World'?"

"Are you raising this as an objection?"

"No. Well, yes, I guess I am. Doesn't God have more important things to do with his time than to run for some political office?"

"What things?"

"World hunger, for instance. Stop all wars. Eradicate poverty. Cure disease. Things that really matter."

"It seems to me" he said, "that you are answering your own question."

Wait. What?

"So, if I understand you correctly, you're saying that before you can address the world's problems, you have to get yourself elected to some political office? I thought the second part of your name was *Almighty!*"

Here I was clearly being derisive.

He calmly responded, "Nothing can happen on earth until

the leader is properly chosen, as you know."

"No, I don't know." I objected, "What does that even mean?"

"You yourselves have a sensible system of electing officials to government office. Usually two candidates are chosen from the field because they are eminently qualified to fill the post. For instance, there is the position of President of the United States. One candidate wins the election and is immediately clothed with immense power and authority, and sets about implementing his agenda for the benefit of the entire nation. The other candidate, equally qualified, goes back to work in the private sector. Just so, nothing can happen on earth until the leader is properly chosen."

"But I thought God was above all that!"

"No, God is not above all that."

"Okay, I'll take your word for it." I decided to humor him. "So, Mr. Christ, how's the campaigning going so far?"

"So far, on the books at least, I have 2.2 billion supporters. But I dare say if the election were held today, a good percentage of those people wouldn't even bother to vote. So you see I still have a good deal of campaigning to do."

"2.2 billion votes?" My jaw has dropped. "Surely that's enough to get you elected, no?"

"The current world population is roughly 7 billion and growing, so even on a good day I could only expect to get 30 percent of the vote, at best. Besides, there's more involved here than just scoring a certain number of votes.

I would like everyone, and by that I mean everyone on earth, to read my campaign literature and make an informed decision based on my record. Also, there are other candidates to contend with."

"I had no idea!"

"Yes, although none of them have formally declared as of yet. I welcome all healthy and legitimate competition for this position. I relish the challenge. The field is wide open. I know many talented individuals who would make fine candidates.

"There is one group, however, influenced by dark occult forces, who does not have the welfare of the planet uppermost in their mind. They are very secretive and extremely powerful. I will hand them a crushing defeat simply by speaking the truth, a strategy that they are entirely ignorant of. My party affiliates refer to them as the ones who are perpetually 'Against Christ'. To me they are nothing but interlopers. But don't get me started on that subject!"

I'm not entirely sure what he is talking about here, but I check my notes and decide to try a different tack:

"That does bring to mind a frequent objection I hear from people who complain that you…" and here I caught myself, "I mean people who complain that the Real Jesus Christ, you know, from way back in time, was too exclusive. He tried to make people think that he, and he alone, could save them."

"Yes," he said, "there is that theme all through my

literature. You may be referring to a speech given by my first campaign manager, Peter, some years back. He stated it emphatically: 'Jesus is the only name under heaven, given to men, by which they can be saved.' and words to that effect. Yes, he was extolling me, and as they say, 'I approve this message.'"

"So then you admit it!"

"Of course! What does any political candidate say about himself? Usually he will say something like 'I am the most qualified, the most experienced, the most well funded, the best educated. I am the only one who can do the job.' Just because a candidate makes these claims about himself doesn't automatically mean the claims are false! He may, in fact, be the best, the only one, who can do the job. In exactly the same way, I am running for the position of President of the World, and I know for a fact that I am uniquely qualified to do the job."

"But where does that leave the poor young girl living in the slums of India who is praying to Buddha to save her? She has never even heard of you."

"Well, Greg, technically that poor young woman from India is probably hoping that *Kalki*, not Buddha, will come and save her, but no matter. Do you really think she is going to object if *I* show up in his place and take her from her misery?"

I had to find a way to unmask this fellow and conduct a sensible interview.

"Okay, Mr. Christ, let's cut to the chase. What exactly do

you think you are going to accomplish as President of the World?"

"Oh, Greg, this is continually on my mind. My heart is breaking. The situation is grave and the hour is late. I see systemic and institutionalized war and violence relentlessly perpetrated on completely innocent people, people who are already stretched to the breaking point. As a journalist yourself, you know that what the media is able to report is just the tip of the iceberg. There is this alarming spread of global terrorism. Good religion has become so distorted that some of these people seriously believe they are acting *in my behalf!* I see human atrocities of unprecedented and unimaginable scope, and widespread starvation, especially of children. Frequent outbreaks of rare or unknown infectious diseases are becoming the norm. I am appalled at the situation. There is a nameless and faceless global economy that is strangling humankind. And then looming over all is the specter of Nuclear Winter, and similar end of days scenarios."

"You can save us from Nuclear Winter?" I asked. His words were so forceful that I was having trouble getting a firm foothold.

"I can save you from Nuclear Winter, or I can rectify the problem after the fact. It's really entirely up to you. By that of course I mean you collectively."

"I happen to think" I said with as much swagger as I could muster, "I happen to think that mankind can solve these problems without any outside help." As soon as the words left my mouth I was ashamed of myself.

"Do I look like a little green creature from Mars?" He seemed affronted.

"No, of course not!" I said. "I meant no disrespect."

"When you refer to mankind, I would appreciate it if you would include me as a member of that species!" His voice rose slightly in pitch.

Wow! Sensitive!

" I guess I just meant that we probably won't require your services as so called 'President of the World'". I thought I should let him down gently. "That just seems so unnecessary and frankly a little overbearing. Come to think of it the concept sounds slightly dangerous and even maybe a little oppressive. Perhaps you should re-think your objectives and set your sights a little lower."

"Greg, can you tell me one country on earth without a recognized leader?"

I thought about this. "No, I can't say that I can."

"Can you tell me one successful corporation or business or human enterprise of any kind that has no recognized leader?"

"Come to think of it, I can't." I said.

"The Earth is a huge ball spinning out in space. It is covered with fractious and disjointed groups of human beings who are collectively destroying each other and everything they touch. It is a situation that is crying out for strong and capable leadership. And the potential for magnificence is so close at hand! I have such great plans for this place, you just wouldn't believe!" His eyes were flashing and his voice was thunderous as he said this.

I am reduced to silence. I look over at this man sitting across from me, and notice for the first time that his suit, a perfectly tailored, very expensive looking fine white linen, is covering what appears to be a powerful body. His neck is thick and muscular. His fingernails are perfectly manicured. I notice with a start that his hands are unusually large. I then remember that I neglected to shave this morning. My shirt is wrinkled, my shoes are scuffed, and I notice an ugly gravy stain on my trousers. Cold sweat is beginning to collect and run down my back. I try to calculate the distance between the door and myself, and realize with a shudder that if I tried to escape he could spring out of his chair like a jaguar and break my neck with his bare hands. I look pleadingly up to his face and find him gazing back at me with a genuine expression of affection!

"Take it easy, Greg." He said. "Have a little courage. It's me. Don't be afraid!"

The trance is instantly lifted, and a strange sense of gratitude comes over me. I suddenly have an almost uncontrollable urge to fall down on my face and grab onto his feet!

When I finally recovered my equilibrium, I looked at my watch and suggested that we pause the interview and pick it up again the next day. He responded enthusiastically, and with that he got up, gave my hand a friendly shake, and walked out the door.

About an hour later a small thin crust veggie pizza was delivered with a note that said, "Please enjoy! J.C."

I opened a cold bottle of water and sat down to a delicious lunch.

My office, as you can imagine, is somewhat old and shabby. But it is surprisingly spacious, with elements of a previous grandeur that hark back to a time when our magazine held national prominence and an extensive readership. The desk, bookcases, and filing cabinets are a rich, dark walnut, finely crafted by A. H. Davenport and Company of Cambridge, Massachusetts. Two genuine Gunlocke high-backed leather chairs, similar to the ones used for years in the White House Oval Office, provide very comfortable seating. A fine old Persian carpet on the hard oak floor and a couple of Tiffany-looking floor lamps add a pleasing ambiance. Unfortunately the original tin ceiling is covered by a dropped acoustical tile affair with glaring florescent light fixtures, which tend to give the room a ghastly sort of pale aspect. Sometimes I just turn them off and use the floor lamps. There is one narrow window in the corner that brings in enough light to show an occasional cobweb or two near the ceiling, and a fine coat of dust over the top of the filing cabinet.

While sitting there eating my lunch my eyes went to a slogan that I had previously tacked to the wall, which read: "With Great Power Comes Great Responsibility" – *Spider-Man*. That watchword has always kind of summed up the extent and depth of my philosophy. Reading the slogan brought me right back to the task at hand. What to do with this guest?

He appeared to be a man with hidden reserves of strength, and even a kind of undefined power. I could see that he was dangerous. But why was he masquerading around like some first century Biblical character? And what were his real motives?

"Power corrupts!" I knew that. "Absolute power corrupts absolutely!" I also thought I knew that. But Spider-man wasn't corrupted, at least not in the final chapters. Abraham Lincoln, a very powerful man, wasn't corrupted. Neither was Theodore Roosevelt, one of my favorite presidents. Nor was my father, for that matter, even though he had absolute power in my family. These were all men who brought their power to bear on the problems at hand, and brought us to a higher, safer place.

One thing I knew: If I was going to keep on top of this interview, I was going to have to go on the offensive big time, and stay there.

DAY TWO

The next morning I intentionally arrived at the office ahead of schedule, but there he was, calmly sitting and waiting for me. Today he was wearing a dark blue running suit and an expensive looking pair of running shoes. I was a little disconcerted because I took the trouble to shower and shave and put on my best suit. Hard to win at this game!

I have come today prepared to test him with some tough religious questions. A man who calls himself Mr. Jesus Christ should be able to shed some light on this topic, I should think.

He began the conversation: "I thought you might like to ask me some of those tough religious questions this morning. Anything in particular on your mind?"

The unnerving process had begun again.

I replied, "Yes. Not to put you on the spot, but I am curious to know how you feel about the Protestant Reformation, and especially the conduct of one Martin Luther!" I don't care one iota about this, but it's the kind of question that seems to get religious people all in a twit.

"He's a good friend of mine." said he.

Hoping to provoke a heated discussion, I pressed on:

"Excuse me, but I am a Roman Catholic (or at least I used to be) and I know that he did a lot of very bad things!"

"Bad things? I'm sorry, but I don't recall these 'bad things.'" he replied.

I knew I had him on the ropes. "You must be aware that he broke his priestly vows and fractured the church and threw the whole western world into a religious chaos!" I heatedly exclaimed.

"You know, Greg, you are an excellent interviewer, much better than you think. Here, in a matter of minutes, you have uncovered my one glaring weakness, if it can be called a weakness. You see I have absolutely no capacity for these 'bad things' you allude to. I just simply have no mind for them. I can't remember them at all. They constitute a blank spot in my brain. They just aren't there at all!"

"On the other hand," he continued, "I can vividly recall every single kind or generous thing that Martin ever did, as if it happened this morning! The tiniest details are crystal clear to me. Love that guy! We have been close friends since the first time we met!"

I could see that this train of thought was going nowhere, so I rolled out the big guns: "What do you have to say about the whole Christian world-view, you know, the old fashioned concept of heaven, hell, and purgatory?"

"That's a very broad topic."

"I hate to say it," I pushed on, "but heaven doesn't seem

all that appealing to me. Maybe it could work for school age children and Catholic Cardinals. But no ordinary grown man is interested in riding around on a cloud all day playing a harp. I would be embarrassed to be caught staying in a place like that."

"Hmm. So the idea of seven billion healthy and attractive singles hanging out in paradise is not your particular cup of tea? You must lead a very exciting life!"

I thought of my typical weekend and muttered something to myself.

"I think you would find heaven fascinating, to tell the truth." He continued. "The people in heaven are very busy. They can't wait to jump out of bed in the morning and get to work!"

"Work? Are you saying we have to work in heaven?"

"Of course! What did you think? We are constantly building, expanding, making improvements. Our current project is adding – you guessed it – seven billion bedrooms onto my father's country house. Seems like the perfect number, doesn't it? This particular project, incidentally, is being carried out entirely with human design, human engineering, human research, human creativity, and human labor. It is really something to see! My father is bursting with pride. He can be seen every day walking through the project, shouting 'Coffee break!' I must say he is a skillful manager."

I can't believe what I am hearing. "Do you mean to tell me that humans are building heaven?"

"Whoa, slow down there, cowboy! I said humans are adding some bedrooms onto my father's country house. Heaven is a very big place and it has been around for a very long time. I only meant to let you know that the whole body of human thought and advancement is appreciated in heaven, and every discipline of art and science and philosophy is continually expanding thanks to the human citizens of heaven. It is of course my desire to incorporate many of our innovations into new housing designs here on earth. Sort of a 'get it done on earth as it is in heaven' approach."

This guy was not giving me the answers I was expecting, that's for sure.

"And Purgatory? What do you have to say about Purgatory?"

"Purgatory is kind of like coming home from work and washing up for a big date. You want to look your best!"

I waited for more on this topic, but that's all he said.

"Okay. Last but not least," I said, "What about Hell? Is there such a place? Does it exist? Do you point your finger at people you don't like and tell them to 'go to Hell'?"

He heaved a little sigh and said, "Many educated people in this day and age have asked themselves whether or not there is intelligent life on other planets, perhaps in other universes, speculating that the laws of chance demand it. I am not going to tell you there isn't. But many of these same people are incredulous when they are told that an alien race of creatures has already landed on their planet!

Yes, a race of enormously powerful and vicious creatures is sharing the planet with you right now, and you are no match for them! H.G. Wells was right on the mark in his famous novel 'War of the Worlds'. Gigantic hideous creatures arrived and simply harvested humans for food by sucking out their blood. This is the situation you currently find yourselves in. If these aliens have one laudable feature, it is their ability to postpone gratification, as long as they know they will get you in the end. High up on my to-do list as governor of this planet is to round up these dogs and lock them up in their self-made torture chamber. That would be Hell, a place they built for themselves to satisfy their insatiable desire for pain and fire. They are not human, Greg, like you and me. I detest their interference in our affairs. I will not tolerate it! Am I getting carried away? I'm sorry, but I feel strongly about this situation." Here he ran his hands through his hair and kind of groaned.

Composing himself, he went on, "What I'm looking for in my administration is a person whom I can call a friend, someone with human qualities, particularly those qualities I mentioned in a campaign speech I made one morning known as 'The Sermon on the Plain'. I would have to say that *mercy* is the one thing I desire most in a person.

"More often than I care to say, I come across an individual who has never, in his whole life, ever displayed even one small act of mercy toward a fellow human being, as hard as that is to believe. When I meet a person like that, we have no basis for pleasant conversation, for friendly banter. We have no repartee. After a few awkward moments and possibly some hostile exchange, that person turns and departs from me. He is, I'm afraid to say, the next meal for one of those vile alien creatures who lurk about in the atmosphere."

At this point I was frantically trying to remember anything I ever did in my whole life that wasn't completely selfish and calculated to my own benefit. Nothing immediately came to mind! In an effort to break the spell and shift the blame, I burst out with:

"You claim that God is all good and is some kind of a father figure to the human race. I can't see why an all-powerful God would plant Adam and Eve in a nice garden, and then set a trap for them, just to see if they would fall in. Tempting them with an apple tree, and then forbidding them to eat apples, seems cruel, sadistic, and perverse!"

"That, my friend, is an excellent question! I was hoping you would ask. Understanding that original exchange is key to understanding the whole progress of human history. You might also say that a clear understanding of the Garden of Eden is the key to good mental health! Yes, that question deserves some looking into. And I will answer you in my own inimitable way! But not today, if you don't mind. Suppose we get together again tomorrow and explore that topic."

With that he got up, spun on his heels, and walked out without even saying "good afternoon".

I completely forgot to thank him for the pizza.

DAY THREE

Almost every night I wake up at least once, at no particular time and for no particular reason as far as I can tell. Normally I just roll over and go right back to sleep.

The third morning of my interview I woke up as usual. The clock read exactly 3:00 am. I rolled over and was preparing to drift back to sleep when I heard a sound in the corner of the room. I opened my eyes and, glory to God, there he was, himself, Mr. Jesus Christ, sitting on the chair by the window! I was so startled that my foot shot out and slammed against the footboard. That action brought me to the dim realization that I had fallen back to sleep and was now dreaming. So I snuggled down into the blankets and let the dream unfold.

Jesus was now standing, and talking into a headset. I couldn't understand anything he was saying until we suddenly made eye contact. He looked at me and said, "I'm so glad you are *here*. You always seem so distant and vague."

Then he went on talking into the headset as he walked around the room, marking all the furniture with colored sticky labels and scribbling notes on a yellow pad. He took out a measuring tape and began measuring everything. He measured the length and width of the room, the height of the ceiling, the distance from the door to the dresser, from the dresser to the chair to the bed to the window. He measured the depth of the water that was flowing across the floor. I was glad to see the water was clear and not muddy. He went over and opened the window, looking out as the breeze ruffled his hair. Then he came over and opened the closet door. He took everything out of the closet and put it all into a large contractor's bag, which he tied and labeled. Picking up the bag, he went to the window and tossed the bag out into the night. I heard a wood chipper in the back yard, so I rolled over and looked at my clock. It was 6:15 am and the alarm was ringing.

I dragged myself out of bed and went to the closet. This morning I decided to stop trying to second-guess the dress code. I put on some comfortable and casual clothes and made my way to the office. Why was I not surprised to find Mr. Jesus Christ waiting there for me, dressed quite casually and comfortably?

We started with the normal pleasantries, then he said, "Today I've decided to tell you a story!"

He must have seen me wince, because he tilted his head and looked at me quizzically.

"Please don't take offense," I said, "Its just that I have heard your stories, or at least the real Jesus' stories, over and over again, and they have a tendency to put me to sleep. I go into a zone. I find myself looking out the stained glass windows and daydreaming."

"Really?" he said, "How odd! How droll! I did come across a fact the other day that I found most interesting. It has to

20

do with sugar maple trees, those brightly colored beauties you see in the autumn. They are valuable, of course, as a source of delicious maple syrup, as well as for their hardwood lumber. What I discovered, however, is that their leaves are highly toxic to horses! Isn't that interesting?"

Why does he think I even care about this trivia?

"Of course," he said, "this is just a bit of trivia for most people, but if you kept horses, it would seem to be a most helpful piece of information!"

Then he began his story:

"There was a wealthy man who lived with his family in Philadelphia. He had a successful law practice and he was active in high political and social circles in the city. He also happened to love horses, and he owned a fine ranch in eastern Tennessee in the foothills of the Great Smoky Mountains. There he bred and exhibited American Saddlebred horses. They were known as the finest show horses in the state.

"So it was that when his son turned eighteen and graduated from high school the man proposed that the boy take a gap year at the ranch before beginning college. 'You can go down there and just soak up the mountain air,' he said. 'Everything runs itself. The foreman and the hands take care of the horses, and the cook and housekeeper run the lodge. I've arranged for you to take riding lessons, and I think you will have the time of your life!

'Just one word of caution. We have planted a stand of young sugar maples in a fenced off area well away from the corral and barn. Keep the horses out of there. Those maple leaves are deadly poison to horses! Other than that, you will be free to roam the wide-open mountain range and have a grand time.'

"The boy left a week later and found everything just as his father had said. The ranch ran itself, and all he had to do was enjoy himself. Taking advantage of his status as 'young master', he quickly got to know everyone on the ranch and everyone in the surrounding countryside, and he was well liked by all. He would frequently take his horse up into the mountains and camp with one or two friends deep in the misty forest. …Greg, hey Greg, are you still with me?"

"What? Oh, sorry. I guess I was daydreaming. The Great Smokies are so majestic. I've been there, you know!"

"Right. One stormy afternoon in the early fall an old ranch hand came over and struck up a conversation with the young man: 'Fine herd of horses your dad has here.'

'Yes they are.' The boy answered guardedly.

'You want to really make them run?' asked the old hand.

'What do you mean?'

'If you feed them wilted maple leaves they will run like the wind!'

'That's crazy!' said the boy. 'Those leaves are poison to horses.'

'Poison? They certainly are not poison! The Indians used to feed maple leaves to their ponies before going to war, and those horses ran like the wind!'

"Not wanting to appear ignorant of Indian lore, and feeling quite the master of his domain, the boy on a sudden impulse led the whole herd of horses into the maple grove and let them feed on the leaves.

"Two days later half the horses on the ranch were dead, and the rest were fighting for their lives.

"Now we had a real situation. The father got the whole story from the foreman, and it would be hard to exaggerate his fury. He was just aghast at the mind-numbing stupidity of the whole affair. He said, 'Tell that kid to pack his bags and get the hell off the ranch before he burns the place to the ground!'

"The boy, of course, was thoroughly ashamed of himself. He could scarcely believe what he had done. But worse than that, he discovered that he was now terrified of his father. The thought of facing his father now was more than he could endure. So he hitched a ride to a different part of the state and kind of went into hiding.

"The secondary fallout was that the local economy practically collapsed with the loss of the ranch and all it entailed. Furthermore, the family's reputation was ruined in that part of the country. The whole scene was a catastrophe!

"Tell me, Greg. Does any of this ring a bell?"

"Yes," I answered, "It does seem to have all the elements of the Adam and Eve story, although in the Bible I don't pick up the intensity of emotions…"

"Well, there was intensity of emotions. You can be sure of that! Adam didn't just kill the horses. He killed every living thing, plant, animal, and human. He subjected all of creation to a slow and painful death! Yes, there was emotion!

"But can we continue our story? Now, this is just a story, Greg. I'm making it up as we go along. My advice is to just relax and try to focus on the big picture."

He must have known I was busily constructing my arguments and planning my next verbal thrust.

"So the father was angry," he continued, "and very disappointed, and crushed at the loss of his beloved horses, and heartbroken at the disappearance of his son. The family was fractured, trust was broken, and there was nothing the father could do. Nor was there anything the son could do, for that matter. Mumbling a lame apology would not replace three hundred thousand dollars worth of prize horses, nor would it restore the family's reputation, nor would it restore the once intimate relationship that they shared.

"The rest, as they say, is history. The boy had an older brother. That would be me! (He added this cryptically.) After about a year the older brother decided to take a leave of absence from his father's law firm and see what he could do, so he packed a duffle bag, threw it in the back of his pickup truck, and headed down to Tennessee. He searched around and eventually found the boy living in a small apartment, working as a handyman. After a tearful reunion, the older brother skillfully mediated a full and satisfying reconciliation between the boy and his father. He then focused his attention on the ranch. Using his own money and employing his considerable skills, he rebuilt the herd of horses, repaired and expanded the ranch, reorganized the business, and brought in his own team of employees. Then he installed his younger brother as manager over the entire operation. Gave him the second chance of a lifetime!

"That could be the end of my story." said my guest. "Would you mind if I added a postscript?"

I could see he wasn't done, so I nodded my head.

"Do you think my story would make sense if I added that the older brother went back to Philadelphia and picked up where he left off at his father's law firm?"

"Of course!" I replied.

"And would it even be remotely conceivable that the older brother eventually got involved in national politics, and made a successful bid for President of the country?"

"Well I suppose that could happen. Yes, of course."

"What effect do you suppose that would have on the younger brother, having a sibling who was President?" he asked.

"Well it couldn't do him any harm!" was my lighthearted reply.

"I'm done with my story, and I've got to get going." He said.

He arose from his chair. His face was flushed and his lips were slightly quivering. Suddenly, without warning, he kind of fell to his knees in front of me, bent over, and wrapped his arms around my ankles! Although the gesture was strangely endearing, I was revolted and thoroughly shocked! This man had no boundaries! He clearly didn't understand the concept of personal space. I hoped to God that no one would enter the room and see us like this. The poor man was becoming unhinged. I was just about to reach for my phone and call Security when he released his hold and got slowly to his feet. Looking at me through moist eyes, he said "Greg, would you mind terribly if we got together one more time, maybe tomorrow morning?"

I checked my busy schedule, and sure enough I had the whole morning free.

DAY FOUR

When I arrived at the office the next morning I was surprised to see that he wasn't there. I took a seat behind my desk and shuffled some papers around, wondering if perhaps the interview was over, after all.

After about ten minutes the door opened and he came in, looking positively disheveled! His hair was rumpled and his eyes looked slightly bloodshot. When he saw me, however, he broke out into a huge smile and came over and shook my hand vigorously. "Greg, it is just a delight to see you this morning!"

I hated to do it, but I knew what I was about to tell him was going to be a huge downer. Instead, I went and got him a large black coffee and a buttered roll, which he accepted eagerly.

"So how are you this morning, Greg?" he asked.

"Well I have some rather disappointing news to report," I began. "The fact is, based solely on your made up story, I went home and did something completely ridiculous and totally uncharacteristic of me. I went up to my room and closed and locked my door. Then I sat on the edge of the bed and spoke right into thin air. I tried to imagine I was talking to 'Father', and I actually apologized for the part I played in causing the world's problems. I was even trying to be sincere for once in my life.

"My words, as I say, went directly up into thin air. I tried to muster a feeling of remorse, a feeling of forgiveness, but it was no use. I could not detect any feeling whatsoever. So I hate to disappoint you, but the practical application of your story seems to have missed the mark totally."

He looked right at me. "No feelings, Greg? No feelings? You may not have felt anything, but my father was absolutely over the moon! He was so jubilant I thought his hair was going to catch fire! He immediately called all of your relatives together, and anyone who might have known you or come in contact with you, and we pulled out all the stops! We have been partying all night! At one point Dad started telling the most hilarious stories about you, and some of your aunts and uncles were practically screaming with laughter! We were literally rolling on the floor! The party just broke up about an hour ago. I apologize for my dreadful appearance."

At this he seemed to recall something, and his whole body began to shake. His face was oddly contorted. It was soon apparent that he was desperately trying to suppress a laugh! It came spilling out in a fit of mirth and he was simply unable to control himself. I got the impression that the joke had to do with me, but his laughter was so infectious that I was soon laughing uncontrollably with him! It took us almost fifteen minutes to regain our composure.

He said, "Oh, Greg, you just have no idea! You just can't imagine!"

Then, doing his best to put on a solemn face, he said, "We

have to get serious. We need to get back to my up-coming election. That's what this interview is all about, after all."

Once again, I felt I had to deliver bad news. "Mister, ah, Jesus" I said, "Uh, are we on a first name basis here?"

"Yes we are, Greg."

"Okay, then. Mr. Jesus, sir, I really don't think this idea of you running for President of the World is going to gain any traction. That's just my opinion."

"Oh no? Why not?"

"For one thing, Jesus Christ has been dead for two thousand years!"

"But you see me here, sitting in this chair across the desk from you. Do I look dead to you?"

"No, but…well, also, if the idea is presented to the general public, most people will glibly say: 'Jesus? President of the World? I don't think so. No thanks!'"

"That response, I dare say, would mostly come from the folks who are presiding over this fiasco," he retorted, " or from the ones who are profiting from it. They constitute a very tiny percentage of my voter base, and I can't let them deter me.

"Do you know," he went on, "that roughly eighty percent of the world's population lives on less than ten dollars a day, many of them on far less? Fifty million people are currently living in refugee camps, lacking in many cases the very basic necessities of life. I seriously doubt any of them would be so quick to dismiss a genuine offer of help! It's just exactly these last who will be first to get the ball rolling."

"You mean to begin the voting process?" I queried.

"Exactly."

Wanting to capitalize on his enthusiasm, I pressed him: "So I'm guessing that everyone will kind of vote for you in his or her heart?"

"I'm happy to have people vote for me in their hearts," he responded, "but what I envision is much more public than that. I envision a kind of grass roots movement, a groundswell that will start small but quickly gain momentum, composed of people who are completely beyond having a sense of humor. Huge masses of people will begin asking, then demanding, then finally compelling their leaders to seek me out and ask me to govern them. All of humankind will finally do something for themselves that makes sense.

"Then, on a day of their choosing in a place that seems acceptable to them, delegates from every nation will meet with me to seal the deal. We will all shake hands and sign some papers and pose for photographs. Perhaps we'll hear a stirring rendition of Verdi's 'Triumphal March' from Aida. Then we'll all go in for a big state dinner. After that we will roll up our sleeves and get to work. Although I'm thinking that Our Father will first insist that everyone take a two week vacation."

I couldn't help myself. Almost jokingly I asked him: "Will

all the nations of the earth see you coming on a cloud, with great power and glory?"

He answered, "I will be arriving on my private plane, and I imagine that everyone will be glued to their TV screens. And there is, I suppose, a measure of power and glory associated with this position. Although considering the amount of work to be done, I believe the glory will fade quickly. So to answer your question, yes, yes, and yes."

Hoping to impress him with my knowledge of scripture, and secretly thinking to catch him in a contradiction, I slyly asked him, "Wait. Aren't you supposed to come like a thief in the night?"

"I am no thief." He answered "And I always work in broad daylight. But I predict that the media, in their normal fashion, will completely ignore the organic process as it develops. And the world leaders will of course try to keep everything under tight wraps until the last possible minute. Word will leak out just days before the big meeting, and then I will finally have the world's undivided attention!"

Once again, I was reduced to silence. I could think of nothing more to say. Finally I yielded. "You are really serious about this, aren't you?"

"Quite serious."

"Well," I stood up and offered him my hand. "Good luck to you. I wish you every success. No, seriously. I've enjoyed meeting you and talking with you and I sincerely hope you achieve your goals."

He arose from his chair and shook my hand. Then he said, "I would like to give you a gift."

"A gift? For me? I really wish you hadn't…"

He asked me to walk around the desk. Then he stood in front of me, looked directly at my forehead, put his hands on my shoulders, and proceeded in a calm voice to recount, one by one, every embarrassing and humiliating thing I had ever done, every vile and selfish and cruel and thoughtless deed, most of which I had long ago forgotten and buried. I found it oddly comforting! The violent ocean storm that normally describes my mind was stilled to a dead calm, like a sailing ship passing through the Doldrums. Then, as if to complete the metaphor, huge tears began to roll out of my eyes, run down my face, and splash noisily on the floor. Other than a sense of peaceful relaxation, I felt nothing at all. It was as if I was a spectator at a mildly interesting stage production. The thought did occur to me that he certainly had no trouble remembering *my* bad things!

Finally he finished up and just stood there a minute. I felt so refreshed. I felt so affirmed!

That's when he hit me right between the eyes! I don't mean literally, of course. He leaned in and said: "I have one last request. How about coming to work for me?"

I was stunned. "Me? Oh, no. No, no, no! I agreed to do this interview, but that's all. I didn't sign on for this. No, I'm afraid not. Absolutely not!"

"Come on, Greg! I could use a guy like you. You're always

looking for something new and different. And I know you're not crazy about your current job. What do you say? I would take good care of you!"

"I just don't think so…"

"Great! I'll take that as a yes!"

I heaved a sigh.

"Your main job" he explained, "will be to talk me up whenever you can. And see if you can get, say, seven billion copies of my gospel campaign literature printed up and passed around everywhere. Lets get this done! And call me every day. I will pick up for you!"

With that, he gave me a big bear hug, shook my hand one last time, then walked around to my side of the desk, sat down in my chair, opened up his briefcase, and began to do some paperwork!

I realized with a start that I was running late for a doctor's appointment, so I quietly backed out of the room and gently shut the door.

PART TWO – AFTERWORD

STRUGGLING WITH MY RESPONSE

If I claimed I "went now in peace" I would definitely be lying. If anything, my mind was more of an ocean storm than ever. Dark confusion seemed to stalk me, and I had an occasional feeling of being physically strangled.

I had a curious little experience one night about three months later. I ducked into a local church to grab a moment of peace and quiet. The church was completely empty except for me. I sat down and whispered a kind of desperate prayer for help. Gradually, almost imperceptibly, I began to feel as if someone were washing me on the inside, sort of scrubbing me. A very peculiar and not unpleasant sensation. That was all. It came and went.

I haven't done a darn thing about campaigning for my new friend Jesus. It has completely gone to the back burner. I did re-read some of his literature, however, with a new set of eyes. To be more precise, I read the entire Bible starting with page one of Genesis straight through to the last page of Revelation. I was particularly interested in the gospel accounts of Jesus. What I discovered there was the description of a man who could set a course of action and stick with it. The man being described also had an uncanny ability to read people's motives. I thought those would be good attributes in a man who aspired to govern. It was also plain to see that everything he did seemed to greatly benefit other people, while he himself often took a beating. There was something solid and gritty about this guy. He stood right up to the big shots and never backed down.

Then there was the preponderant sense of some kind of ongoing cosmic struggle. On the one hand Jesus spent a lot of time expressing a desire to save us and *feed* us, whereas his nemesis was always out to kill us and *eat* us. No wonder the human race is a little psychotic.

I looked into the world population statistics that he spoke about. There are about 7.2 billion people on the planet as of 2014. About 6 billion of them live in less developed countries. Almost 1 billion of them are totally illiterate, many more are barely literate, and over half the total population on earth is less than 30 years old. So I have to conclude that an enormous number of people on earth have never even heard about Jesus Christ, or have minimal accurate information about him. And in some large regions of the globe, the population is forcibly prevented from even reading his literature at all, under pain of imprisonment or death.

Nevertheless, I have seen strange things happen when groups of people get stirred up and things go viral. It is entirely possible that the frustration level could reach such proportions that a global revolution could work in his favor. I ask myself if it were put to a fair vote, who else, really, would anybody vote for?

Well, that's my opinion, anyway.

I am still haunted by his request that I come to work for him. When I first met him I thought that he was completely out of his mind, particularly when he fell at my feet weeping on that day in my office. Over the past months however I have come to the inescapable conclusion that we are living in a world that is *itself* out of its mind. More and more each day. Some of us could actually be compared to a herd of demon-possessed pigs running headlong over a cliff and drowning in the sea!

Even so there are many, really millions, of highly educated and intelligent people who are doing their absolute best to pull things together, and they are doing a great job in their particular fields of expertise.

But there aren't more than ten people on the entire planet who really know what needs to be done to fix the world.

I am one of those ten people.

Not because I am so smart. Not at all! I only know what to do because he told me: "Print up seven billion copies of my gospel campaign literature and pass them out everywhere."

He said it in such an offhand manner that I really didn't attach much significance to it. But after reflecting I can see that his plan is the most common-sense approach to getting him elected to the office he seeks. And that, I believe, is the key to fixing the world that we live in.

But the idea that I could achieve this is ridiculous! Who does he think I am? I can't possibly fulfill his request. I wouldn't even know where to begin.

I know there is something I need to do, but I don't know what it is. I'm in a proverbial pickle. Perched on the horns of a dilemma.

Basically he threw my life into turmoil. Why did he have to show up in the first place? I was happy going about my business before he got involved.

And yet, I believe I would trade my entire former existence for a few more uncomfortable hours with him.

Give me a little time; I'll come up with something…

PART THREE – MY WEBSITE

LET'S GET THIS DONE!

I have decided to cast aside doubt and courageously launch a website, shooting for the stars! And why not? Who knows what might come of it?

The goals of my website are simple:

1. Put a copy of the gospel into the hands of every single person living on the face of the earth, and
2. Get Jesus elected President of the World by a democratic process of popular vote by paper ballot.

These seem like reasonable goals that can be implemented with a little focused attention and some cooperation from willing individuals.

You may continue reading this story by going to your computer and typing in the link:

www.letsgetthisdone.siterubix.com.

See you on the other side!

PAGE ONE – HOME PAGE

Thank you for visiting my website.

It's great to have you here. As you may know, this website is a continuation of my short story "An Interview With Jesus Christ". For reasons that I outlined in that story, I am interested in promoting the distribution of small gospel campaign booklets on a global scale, with the ultimate intention of getting Jesus elected to the position of President of the World.

Of course this is not a new idea. There are many organizations already in existence that are focused on similar objectives. My feeling is that another voice can only help the cause. Besides, I may have some fresh ideas that could be of use to the many well-organized and highly dedicated individuals engaged in this effort.

I should mention right up front that I am not talking about the process of *evangelization*. *Evangelization* has to do with signing up for life, changing my behavior, letting my mind be renewed, and following a brand new course of action. That is not a bad thing, but that is not what this website is about. My concern *here* is to campaign for my candidate, and get him elected to office. That's the whole focus of this website.

There are many who would say that politics and religion are a bad mix, and that there should be a strict separation between church and state. I get that. My object is to keep the two separate, as much as possible, and concentrate exclusively on the campaign. However, there will inevitably be some crossover due to two factors:

1. Jesus is who he is, and he probably won't change for the likes of me, and
2. The church itself has a definite political component. The church is just like every other political party in as much as it is doing everything it can to promote its candidate.

A Worldwide Campaign

I am also interested in demonstrating that the process of conducting a worldwide campaign of this nature does not have to be complicated or expensive or intimidating.

In fact, I propose to put forth a plan that anyone can easily participate in with practically no effort or inconvenience.

If you're with me, then...

Let's Get This Done!

PAGE TWO – OUR CAMPAIGN BROCHURE

(INCLUDING THE VOTER BALLOT)

The General Idea

What I think may be helpful is a printing of the gospel of Mark (or any of the four gospels), without any annotations or chapter headings or verse numbering or any other **paratext**, similar to the way it's presented in many church missalettes. Just a straightforward narrative, printed on inexpensive white paper with a simple unmarked cover, and packaged in a brown sealed envelope.

Why the Gospel of Mark?

The gospel of Mark is the shortest of the Gospels. Some say it is the most straightforward. The U S Conference of Catholic Bishops has this to say about the gospel of Mark:

"This shortest of all New Testament gospels is likely the first to have been written, yet it often tells of Jesus' ministry in more detail than either Matthew or Luke. It recounts what Jesus did in a vivid style, where one incident follows directly upon another. In this almost breathless narrative, Mark stresses Jesus' message about the kingdom of God now breaking into human life as good news and

Jesus himself as the gospel of God. Jesus is the Son whom God has sent to rescue humanity by serving and by sacrificing his life."

Why no Paratext?

The objective would be to provide a first time reader with a simple account of Jesus' public life. An uncomplicated and forthright presentation could serve for a better reception of his candidacy, a clearer understanding of who he is, what he stands for, and why he is running for office. The words flow nicely by themselves and the verse numbers and commentary aren't really needed at this point. Here's a good example of the kind of thing Jesus would talk about, in plain language:

Jesus said to them, "Do you not understand this parable? Then how will you understand any of the parables? The sower sows the word. These are the ones on the path where the word is sown. As soon as they hear, Satan comes at once and takes away the word sown in them. And these are the ones sown on rocky ground who, when they hear the word, receive it at once with joy. But they have no root; they last only for a time. Then when tribulation or persecution comes because of the word, they quickly fall away. Those sown among thorns are another sort. They are the people who hear the word, but worldly anxiety, the lure of riches, and the craving for other things intrude and choke the word, and it bears no fruit. But those sown on rich soil are the ones who hear the word and accept it and bear fruit thirty and sixty and a hundredfold."

It would be better in my opinion if the booklet cover and the envelope had no title or identifying marks to

reveal their content.

Simply exercising some caution, an unmarked copy of the gospel booklet might be more likely to avoid detection in a geographic location where the mere possession of the gospel would be considered a capital offense, often punishable by death. The booklet I envision might easily be overlooked by hostile authorities. In case of extreme and imminent danger, a small booklet of this type could be hastily burned or destroyed without being discovered.

Even in a less dangerous situation there may be prejudice or resistance to the distribution of any part of the Bible. Unmarked packages could therefore be more easily delivered where they are most needed, without interference.

If the booklet, or the envelope, needs to be marked for identification, it could be stamped with the words,

Let's Get This Done!

The package containing our little booklet is about the size of a small package of garden seeds.

Voter Ballot

I propose that a voter ballot be inserted as the last page of the gospel booklet to encourage the reader to make a simple private choice for Jesus.

OFFICIAL BALLOT

Anywhere on Earth

INSTRUCTIONS: After you have read the Gospel of Mark and have carefully considered the public record of Jesus Christ, please answer the following question:

Would you vote for Jesus Christ as

President/Governor of the World?

Yes I Would

No I Would Not

Comments:

Signature_____

Date_____

Please keep this ballot in a safe place.

How would these gospel booklets be delivered?

I initially considered enlisting the services of Bible couriers, those individuals or groups who deliver Bibles free to anywhere on earth where they are wanted. But for the purposes of political expediency I've decided to abandon that idea for the time being. Couriers serve mostly isolated Christian communities, and as such they are delivering Bibles to people who have already *voted* for Jesus.

Of course, the focus could change for these organizations once the campaign heats up in earnest. We may find ourselves working side by side sometime in the near future. I've included a list of some prominent Bible couriers here, for informational purposes:

International Bible Givers (IBG) is a group of volunteers with a passion for giving free Bibles to whoever needs one – locally, regionally, nationally, and around the world.

Revival Chinese Ministries International. They desperately need copies of the bible for home churches in rural China. They are asking for 35,000 copies, but they could probably use ten times that many.

Voice of the Martyrs and its affiliates are active in about 50 countries, caring for, equipping, supporting and encouraging persecuted Christians, which includes Bible placement.

The American Bible Society. "We provide God's Word to hard-to-reach places, bringing hope across barriers of geography, translation, oppression and injustice."

A Wider Involvement. Once the campaign gets underway it is safe to say that many volunteers will come forward and ask to participate. Not just party members, but others as well, will be asking to play a part, and of course everyone's help will be needed and appreciated. We are talking about a global effort!

On the next page I will explore our political strategy, and the delivery process that I am endorsing.

PAGE THREE – OUR POLITICAL STRATEGY

One day I approached Jesus and asked, "What if, after all our effort, the unthinkable happens? What if the world leaders conduct an honest, straightforward, above board, democratic election, and you lose? Suppose someone else is elected? Suppose you are defeated? **Suppose you are rejected?"**

I expected a look of alarm, a crack in his confidence, but he was completely blithe, totally unconcerned. He shrugged his shoulders and said, "That's politics! Business as usual! I'll just go back to work in the private sector like every other defeated candidate. There's no dishonor in losing a well-run campaign. And I certainly have plenty to do running my non-profit!"

"But", he said, "I am a patient man, and determined! There will be other campaigns and other elections. I don't plan to give up. My father used to encourage me when I was younger. He would say, 'Advance! Advance!' Sooner or later I will be victorious."

The Political Campaign of Jesus Christ

Spreading small gospel booklets all over the globe can certainly be considered a political campaign, which indeed it is! Jesus is interested in governing the planet earth with his feet on the ground and his headquarters on dry land. A case could be made that Jesus' first visit here was to build a political organization (The Church) and to kick off his campaign by making speeches and demonstrating his very impressive and unique skill set!

What are the requirements of a political campaign?

In order to be recognized as a viable entity, a political organization must have certain attributes:

- A political campaign needs a candidate who is qualified for the position. Done.
- The candidate must have a proven track record. Done.
- The candidate must have a loyal following. Done.
- The candidate must have an organization in place. Done.
- The candidate must be able to withstand adversity. Done.
- **The candidate must try to win the hearts and minds of the people.**

It is this last qualification that we are focusing on. Jesus needs to win the hearts and minds of the people.

What is Jesus' Current Standing?

The world's population is roughly 7 billion people. Of those, 2.2 billion claim to be Christian. So Jesus' current standing is **approximately 30 percent** of the total world population.

In order to win this type of election democratically, Jesus would need at least a respectable majority. At a minimum he would need **another 1.3 billion supporters.** He hasn't indicated his exact criteria for a political victory, but that would be a good target, a good starting point.

A good campaign needs a good campaign slogan, and this is ours:

Let's Get This Done!

Jesus Christ For President of the World

What tools do we have at our disposal to help win the hearts and minds of the voters?

We have a vast arsenal of art and music and literature and history to work with. These aids have been packaged and delivered in every conceivable form and fashion, and have been enormously beneficial. They continue today to have a huge impact on world thought and opinion. Their use in our campaign is invaluable.

However, the single most effective tool that we have, more powerful by far than all the rest, is the **simple printed gospel.**

The Gospel as Seed.

This is a topic that ties in perfectly with our campaign to spread gospel packages around the world with a view towards achieving political victory.

Jesus himself uses the example of **seed** at least four times in the course of delivering his numerous speeches:

1. He talks about a farmer who sows **seed** on different types of soil with varying success;
2. He mentions a farmer who sows his **seed**, and then stands back and watches it develop over time until it is ripe;
3. He speaks of a tiny **seed** that produces a surprisingly large bush;
4. He reminds us that a seed remains a **seed** until it is planted, whereupon it undergoes a transformation and produces a useful crop.

All of this is common knowledge and is well known to every weekend gardener. What's interesting is his particular application. He makes a strong case that a small book or a collection of speeches can behave in exactly the same way as a common garden seed. One could even say that he was hinting, or even strongly suggesting, that his campaign be carried out as though it were an agricultural enterprise. Furthermore, he is pretty blunt about his analogy: **"The seed is the word of God"**.

Applying the Analogy

Applying his analogy to the task at hand, we can make some observations, touching on each of his four examples:

1. If the gospel is a seed, then people are obviously the soil:

- We've got sanguine, melancholic, phlegmatic, choleric.
- We've got analysts, diplomats, sentinels, explorers.
- We've got Blacks, Whites, Asians, Hispanics, Others.
- We've got republicans, democrats, libertarians.

- We've got communists, socialists, capitalists, fascists.
- We've got Christians, Muslims, Hindus, Jews, Buddhists, Taoists.
- We've got 1st world, 2nd world, 3rd world.
- We've got upper class, middle class, lower class.
- We've got literate and illiterate.
- We've got healthy. We've got sick.

All of these people constitute good "soil". This is our voter base. These are the people to whom we make our pitch. None should be disqualified. The results of our work will only come to light after a lapse of time. Which ties into the second point:

2. After sowing our seed, or in this case distributing our gospel booklets, we lose control of the process, so to speak. Things begin to happen of their own accord, while we go about our business. In fact, the less we interfere at this point, the better. Let nature take its course. Perhaps a program of polling could give an indication of how successful we have been: public opinion polls, online polls, live-interview polls and the like. But the germination and growth and development of the gospel seed is a thing that happens mysteriously within each individual.

3. We should not be ashamed or abashed at our meager offering: A **plain and simple 20-page booklet.** (i.e. the gospel of Mark.) What impact can such a middling little tract really have? But we are assured that even a tiny package like that can produce a surprisingly large result. This particular item is packed with enormous, game-changing power!

4. A gardener knows that a seed packet stored in the shed needs to eventually be taken out and planted in the garden.

Similarly, if we have crates of published gospel booklets safely stored away in a warehouse we have only done half the job. We've got to get them properly distributed.

A logical approach would be to identify a nice field, and then methodically sow the seed in an organized manner until that field is properly and completely sown. *Done! Move on to the next field!*

This is the essence of our campaign strategy.

For instance, in the People's Republic of China, in the Anhul Province, there is a prefecture level city there called Huangshan. Huangshan City is made up of three districts and four counties. One of those districts, the **Tunxi** district, forms the central part of the city itself.

Tunxi district has a population of 150,000 people. It covers an area of approximately 96 square miles, roughly 10 miles long by 10 miles wide. It is located near an area of breathtaking natural beauty, where the movie "Avatar" was partially filmed! The district itself boasts of some charming ancient architecture. This might make a perfect first field to plant!

This would require the delivery of 75,000 copies of our small gospel booklet, possibly to one or more of the several established Christian churches right there in Tunxi. With the help of the local Christians or other interested volunteers, how long would it take to hand deliver copies to each individual address? Let's assume that 150 people each took responsibility for 500 copies. Two copies would go to each household of four people, so each volunteer would need to deliver to 250 addresses. In a compact city of that size it might not take more than a week to ten days.

There! One field completely sown! Let's check that one off our list and move on to another promising field, say in Balurghat, West Bengal, India, population 150,000.

Our campaign is well under way!

PAGE FOUR -
ADVERTISING/FUNDRAISING

As I may have mentioned, every now and then Jesus will just drop in on me, unannounced. It happened one day while I was sitting at an outdoor cafe down the street from my office. It was late afternoon on a warm day in July. The sky was mostly cloudy, and it looked like it might rain any minute. My thoughts, like the weather, were fairly gloomy. Suddenly he just appeared out of the crowd, came over, and took a seat.

I was happy to see him, of course, and we chatted awhile. But for some reason, I felt irritated. He seemed to have everything going for him. He was rich, powerful, self-satisfied (or so I imagined). And here I was, wracking my brain, trying to accomplish something for him, while he appeared completely aloof! I glanced down at his shoes and saw that he was wearing a pair of exquisitely fashioned alligator wingtips. That really put me in a funk. This guy was just *using* me!

Whack!

It felt as though someone had smacked the back of my head with a cane. But when I looked up, Jesus had not moved from where he was sitting. He scowled at me and said, "Get a grip, Greg!"

Then, softening his glance, he said, "You can look down, or you can look up. You can be discouraged, or you can be encouraged. You can decide that this campaign is hopeless and foolish and childish, or you can see the glorious possibilities! I recommend that you have a little faith. Fix your mind on a positive outcome! Try to imagine victory, visualize success…

"You like these shoes? Here, take them."

With that he slipped off his shoes and pushed them toward me with his foot.

I felt foolish, and objected, but he insisted. "Give me those old scuffed up loafers. They look fine to me!"

So I put on his shoes, and they looked terrific, I must say. I couldn't wait to show them off to my friends.

And with the shoes came a magical surge of creativity. Suddenly I had all sorts of crazy ideas flowing through my mind, most of them totally impractical, of course. But who cares?

Jesus smiled, and with that he rose to his feet, saluted me military style, and went on his way.
As I watched him walk away, I thought I saw him limping slightly. Those shoes were never that comfortable. Not only that, but from the back he appeared a little bent over, as if he were battling discouragement. I felt sorry for him.

My new shoes were certainly very nice!

And then a wave of wonder swept over me. Could it possibly be that he was battling my discouragement, as he limped away in my shoes? No, that would just be inconceivable. And yet, that was the clear impression that settled in my mind.

I love that guy! I just love him! I'm not slaving for him at all. That afternoon I really felt for the first time that we were working together as a team.

A sudden gust of wind scattered paper cups all over the sidewalk, as people ran for cover. A blinding flash of lightning, a crack of thunder, and a minute later the skies opened up and the rain came pouring down.

The street became deserted. The rain increased in volume.

I sat there glued to my seat, lost in some sort of ecstatic fantasy.

I'm thinking of a giant billboard with a yellow banner screaming:

Let's Get This Done!

Next to the banner, in huge letters,

JESUS CHRIST FOR PRESIDENT OF THE WORLD

Envision one of these giant billboards on the main artery into any of the world's great cities!

Tokyo.

Delhi.

Mexico City.

Mumbai.

Sao Paulo.

Beijing.

New York.

Cairo.

Managing such an enormous undertaking would of course be entirely beyond my scope. Hopefully some wealthy individual or non-profit trust will see the value of this advertising campaign and make it their own.

Our Campaign Should Be Conducted In The Normal Fashion:

Buttons, bumper stickers, pens, tee-shirts, coffee mugs, with our campaign slogan plastered all over the place. Newspaper ads, TV commercials, feature articles, media hype to the max.

How about a 5K run as a fundraiser?

 Marathons, half-marathons, tri-athalons, 5K's, walk-a-thons. Everyone loves them, and everyone comes out a winner.

A well organized race in a small city could net up to $30,000 in sponsorships. (The out of pocket expenses are normally covered by the runner's entry fee.)

So here we go with the math: Let's say every race nets $25,000, on the conservative side. How many cities are there in the world? **According to the World Atlas,** there are 4,416 cities in the world with a population of at least 150,000 people. These would be considered relatively small cities.

If 4,416 small cities ran well organized 5K fundraisers, the total net profit would be an impressive...**$110 million dollars!**

PAGE FIVE - HOW MUCH WILL IT COST?

How Much Money Is There?

Perhaps a good question to start with is, "How much money is there? What are we talking about here?" This is a pertinent question since we are, after all, discussing an election that is to take place on a global scale. This election will change the course of human history and be a lasting benefit to the entire human race. There are 2.2 billion Christians who already know this, even if no one else does. So we need to know where we stand financially.

The amount of money that can be spent has been quantified by economists and financial people and is designated by the term **M2. M2** is made up of cash, paper money and coins, or currency, as well as all the money in checking and savings accounts and money market accounts. It's money that can be spent and it equals roughly 60 trillion dollars. That does not include long term investments and other tied up money. So we have approximately 60 trillion dollars at our disposal. That's $60 followed by twelve zeros. It's not as if this money is being used up, either. At the end of the month, after everyone has paid their bills, there is still the same amount of money left. It has just been passed around a bit. Next month, after everyone has paid their bills again, the money is still there, and so forth. Really, the money can be spent again right after the checks have cleared the bank, two or three business days. So we have plenty of money on hand.

How much is it going to cost to print up seven billion copies of the gospel?

I checked online to see how much a Bible costs. Printers are able to print the entire Bible these days for as little as $5.00 per copy.

These same printers are able to offer the entire New Testament for as little as $1.50 per copy.

I am willing to bet that a publisher would be able to print a streamlined version of a single gospel for as little as $1.00 per copy. This of course works out to a mere $7 billion dollars for our project.

How many copies do we really need?

The earth's population is about 7 billion souls total. If 2 billion already belong to our party, then we only need to address the remaining 5 billion who are not affiliated with us. Assuming that half of them are children, we only need to print 2.5 billion gospel booklets, one for each adult.

Just to be on the safe side, and to account for the inevitable loss, damage, and unforeseen difficulties that come up, I propose that we stick to our original target of 7 billion copies.

The total cost of our project is $7 billion.

If my math is correct, 7 billion people could be supplied with our little campaign booklet for a total cost of $1.00 per person. Every person should throw in a buck. Fair is fair.

However, in the world of politics, no one would even dream of paying to purchase a piece of campaign literature. It would be preposterous for us to expect that.

So it remains incumbent upon our party to supply literature, free of charge, to all those we hope to engage.

If each adult party member (there are 1 billion adult Christians on the books) contributes his or her fair share, the total, one time individual campaign contribution is:

$7

This would not be a tithe, or a monthly offering, or a yearly tax, or a recurring payment. This would be a single, lifetime contribution. It could be given all at once, or it could be given over a period of seven years, at a dollar a year, or over the course of a person's entire lifetime. As long as it adds up to $7 dollars, that person would have contributed his or her fair share, in full. For many this might represent a sizable amount, and others could come forward to make up the deficit. But $7 dollars each is the total monetary cost of pre-election world canvassing.

But wait! I foresee a difficulty here. Even well intentioned Christians have a limit. The sheep, as they say, have been fleeced, and before the wool grows back they are fleeced again! No one objects too much, but a line has to be drawn. I feel uncomfortable asking these people for money.

Where am I going to get the money for this project?

I have to stop thinking church, and go back to thinking *campaign*.

I went online, and typed in "how to run a political campaign", and what I found surprised me:

The majority of the work related to fundraising is the responsibility of the *candidate!*

Bingo! I am off the hook! It is up to Jesus to make the speeches and raise the cash!

I considered this a little more, and it makes perfect sense. First of all, I've been a member of several political parties over the years, and I can't ever remember anyone expecting me to make a donation. My own party sends me free campaign literature! Who is paying for this? It's certainly not the rank and file party members.

In the world of politics, a successful candidate turns to **corporate sponsors** and **wealthy individual donors** with bundles of cash, you know, lying around their houses. This is where the money has to come from for printing up our campaign literature. And as I pointed out, there is no lack of available money.

PAGE SIX - THE SUMMARY

In November 2014, I was granted an exclusive interview with Jesus Christ, which was chronicled in the first part of this book. At the end of the interview, Jesus asked me to come work for him in his ongoing campaign to become elected **President of the World.**

My mandate was explained in these words, *"See if you can get, say, seven billion copies of my* **gospel campaign literature** *printed up and passed around everywhere. Let's get this done!"*

So the purpose and intention of this website is to promote the production of "campaign literature" size copies of the gospel for distribution everywhere in the world where they can do some good. *Seven billion* roughly represents the current world population as of 2014.

Here is a key factor:

1. Simple economically printed copies of a single gospel can be mass- produced for $1.00 each or less.

How many copies do we really need?

1. In our pursuit of world canvassing, we could probably get by with printing 2.5 billion copies of

the gospel, one copy for each non- affiliated adult now living on the planet.
2. Just to be on the safe side, and to account for the inevitable loss and damage and unforeseen circumstances, **we should strive to print the entire 7 billion copies.**

How much is this going to cost?

1. $7 billion dollars will neatly cover the cost of printing our campaign brochures. Raising the money is the responsibility of the candidate, in this case Jesus. He will solicit donations from corporate sponsors and wealthy individuals.

What is my involvement?

1. I will be hosting this website to explain my plan and to invite any willing publishers to participate.
2. Those individuals or corporations who are sending donations to a publishing house should write the name of this website on their check, or on the envelope, or on a slip of paper. The name of the website is
www.letsgetthisdone.siterubix.com.
3. A publisher would then be prompted to reference my website and consider the wisdom of my plan.
4. I have **no understanding or agreement** with any publisher.

Fine Points of the Plan:

1. The gospel to be printed would be the **gospel of Mark,** the shortest and most straightforward of the gospels.

2. It would be **printed as a simple narrative,** without comments or footnotes or explanations, and without verse numbers or chapter titles.
3. The gospel would be **sealed in a plain brown wrapper** with the words "Lets Get This Done!" printed on the outside.
4. A simple **voter's ballot** would be placed at the end, with the question: "Would you vote for this man as president of the world? Check Yes or No. Signature and date."
5. The gospel packets would be **methodically delivered, city by city, across the entire earth,** mainly by local volunteers.
6. Once the gospels have been successfully delivered to everyone on earth, **we should wait a reasonable amount of time**, perhaps three or four months, for the voters to decide.
7. We would then **systematically collect the paper ballots** and tabulate them, a process to be carried out by trustworthy individuals chosen by the local populace in every geographic location.
8. **If** we can collect roughly 4 billion authentically signed affirmative ballots, we have a clear democratic majority. The election is won, and our campaign is a success.
9. **Jesus will gladly show up** and assume control of the planet.

So let's get this done!

PAGE SEVEN - A LIST OF BIBLE PUBLISHERS

As soon as sufficient money is made available, we need to select a publisher and begin producing our gospel booklets.

I have compiled a short list of Bible publishers that we could use. Here they are:

1. The American Bible Society
2. Biblica
3. Wycliff
4. United Bible Societies
5. Gideons International
6. Baronius Press
7. St. Benedict Press
8. Tyndale House
9. Zondervan
10. Lutheran Braille Workers, Inc.
11. Crossway
12. Multi Language Media

These people are all professionals. They are in the business, and they are very good at what they do.

They all, more or less, have the same business model:

1. They will sell you a Bible, or
2. They will give you a Bible if your circumstances are dire and you request a free copy.

In other words, if a person wants a Bible, these publishers will gladly deliver it to him.

So we could select any one of these printers, and purchase as many gospel packages as we need.

Unfortunately, the people these companies are focusing on and supplying are not at all the demographic we are aiming at during this campaign.

We are concentrating on people who **Do Not Want the Gospel!**

- **They have never heard of such a thing as a gospel,**
- **Or they are way too busy earning a living and raising their children, and the gospel seems irrelevant,**
- **Or they have already promised to vote for someone else and therefore believe their minds are made up.**

They don't have a pressing desire for the gospel. They certainly would not buy a copy of the gospel, or ask for a copy, or even think about the gospel.

We want to pursue these people because our campaign is seeking **new votes**. It's the new votes that are going to bring our numbers up.

I was hoping to find a Bible publisher who was interested in aiming specifically at these people. I think I may have found one. It is a small organization called **Lock Haven Scripture Press**. These people really have the idea, in my estimation!

1. They post surprising, eye-opening statistics about the distribution of the gospel, and
2. They extol the intrinsic worth of small, semi-autonomous missionary churches.

Both of these features caught my eye because they seem to dovetail perfectly with our campaign strategy.

So although the large companies are excellent and capable and dependable, wouldn't it be nice to throw some of our business toward a small outfit with a big heart and a kindred spirit?

A NOTE TO WEALTHY DONORS, CORPORATE SPONSORS, AND GENEROUS INDIVIDUALS:

Would you do me the favor of mentioning my website when you contact one of these publishing companies?

Please copy and clip the following form and send it along with your substantial contribution:

To whom it may concern:

I am a supporter of the "Let's Get This Done!" campaign to elect Jesus Christ "President of the World".

Please accept my contribution to be used for the publication and distribution of the gospel of Jesus in this ongoing effort.

If you would like more information on this unique presidential campaign, please visit the website:

letsgetthisdone.siterubix.com

Thanks for doing an excellent job!

THIS CONCLUDES MY PLAN FOR A WORLDWIDE CAMPAIGN TO ELECT JESUS CHRIST PRESIDENT OF THE WORLD

I received a memorandum from corporate headquarters:

My employer was pleased with the way I conducted our recent interview with Jesus Christ, and the owners of the magazine requested that I be assigned to cover his campaign as it begins to unfold.

My instructions were to make myself available to Jesus, but not to stalk him or badger him like some obnoxious paparazzi. Jesus would contact me at his own leisure whenever he needed me.

Furthermore, I was instructed to post my experiences on this very website whenever some event occurred.

***

My first campaign excursion took place last night, and my first post can be found on the following pages.

PART FOUR – POSTS

CAMPAIGNING WITH JESUS

POST # 1 - PUB CRAWLING WITH JESUS CHRIST

Last night Jesus showed up at my apartment and said, "Get your coat. We're going campaigning."

By now I was used to his spontaneous ways and his persuasive style. So I got my coat, and off we went, straight down the street and into the first bar we came to.

The place was packed and we squeezed our way to a couple of bar stools that had just been vacated. On the way over a big lug of a guy ran smack into Jesus, and hollered, "Watch it, bud!" It was clearly his fault, but Jesus let it go.

Somehow this same big lug landed on the bar stool next to mine. I read his tee shirt. It said, "Drinking is my religion.

Care to join me in a prayer?" He leaned over and said, "Who's your fine and fancy friend?"

I said, "You might be surprised to discover that he is a candidate for very high political office!"

Well, with that he launched into a tirade the likes of which I had never heard, with a vocabulary that cannot be printed on a page. The gist of what he was saying amounted to: "There is no such thing as an honest politician. God has not made that man yet."

At this, Jesus reached across, put out his hand, and said, "Hi. I'm Jesus Christ."

The big fellow let out a terrific laugh and said, "Glad to meet you. I'm the Pope!"

"No," said Jesus, "You're Jerry Donovan, from over on 3rd Street. I knew your mother Eunice."

The big man temporarily took on the appearance of a pillar of salt.

Jesus rose to his feet, turned his back to the bar, and said in a loud voice that could be heard over the din of the crowd and the clinking of glasses, "I'm buying drinks for everyone tonight! Whatever you want! All night!"

The place went instantly silent. Someone switched off the TVs. You could hear a pin drop.

Then a fellow in the back cheered, and everyone began to clap and shout their approval. They were a lively crowd, and thirsty!

Jesus turned to me and asked in a low voice, "Do you have any money?"

I nearly soiled my pants right then and there.

He laughed, stuck his hand in his pocket, and pulled out a sizeable wad of cash. Handing it to me he said, "Would you do me a favor and see if you can find the owner of this place?"

By the time I returned from that errand, Jesus was sitting at a table smack in the center of the room, with everyone else crowding around him in a large circle, telling stories and jokes, and toasting him and each other. Within fifteen minutes he knew everyone by first name, and a funny fact about each person.

He cleared his throat, put his hands in his pockets, rocked back slightly in his chair, and said, "I suppose you all know the one about Samvar Sadangi?"

We all agreed that we did not.

"Really? That's one of the favorites where I come from."

And so he began:

"There was a boy born in India whose mother was sick and unable to care for him. So she gave him to a fine young Hindu couple who raised him lovingly as their own son.

"Sam was lavished with good things. He had school mates and cousins and children from the neighborhood to play with, and everything he could possibly need or desire.

"But Sam was discontent. As a teenager he took normal rebellion to a whole new level. He chose the greatest Hindu festival to announce to his parents that he was a Vampire, and soon he began to suck the blood out of them, almost literally. His demand for things was insatiable, and to capture everyone's attention he began to fake suicide attempts. Since these had to be taken seriously, the family spent their entire fortune on hospitals and rehabs and powerful psychotic drugs. The pressure on his parents was so unbearable that their marriage ended in a humiliating divorce. Sam took advantage of this new vulnerability by stepping up his demands even further, insisting that they buy him a brand new Harley Davidson Road King, without the slightest thought of how they were going to pay for it. When family friends tried to talk some sense into him he cursed them viciously and spread wild rumors about them. Taking all the money he could get his hands on, he went on a wild and completely deranged cross-country spree of booze, sex, and drugs. Finally, he settled down somewhere way out in the country.

"One day Sam died.

"He found himself in a large open foyer, with numerous people milling about, and presently a door opened and in walked The Enlightened One, Lord Vishnu.

"Lord Vishnu called to Sam, and invited him to take a seat, so Sam came over trembling and sat down.

"Lord Vishnu said, 'Sam, I remember one thing about you. I remember the time, you remember, when you ran into Raj Patel. He was dirty and broke and strung out on drugs. I clearly recall that you took him to your apartment and let him use your shower, and got him something to eat, and gave him some clean clothes. And when he left several days later you didn't even mind that he had stolen some money from your wallet. You figured he needed it more than you did. I remember all this because Raj's parents were friends of mine, and we were quite worried about him. So for that reason, I would like to have you come and live with me.'

"Several of the lawyers standing nearby strongly cautioned against this course of action, citing bad example and dangerous precedent. But Lord Vishnu had the last word, and it came to pass."

Jesus asked, "Does anyone know the point of this story?"

No one had the slightest clue.

"You've all done shameful and selfish things in your life. All can be forgiven, and the sooner the better. What really catches my interest, however, are those spontaneous and generous acts of kindness and mercy that come to my attention. They really stand out in my mind. They give me something I can work with! Yes, I am searching for acts of mercy, or even just an attempt at mercy. That trumps everything in my book!"

Then Jesus stood up, climbed up on the chair, raised his right hand, and said, "I am running for President of the World. Can I count on your support?"

Every hand in the place, including Jerry Donovan's, shot straight up in the air.

POST # 2 – OFF TO SWITZERLAND

Five thirty in the morning. Jesus is standing at my door, knocking.

"Get dressed! We have a plane to catch!"

I began to fumble around with the coffee pot, but he said, "No time! Taxi is waiting!"

So off we went to God knows where.

We got on a plane bound for Switzerland, and in six hours we were there.

On the way, to kill time, we caught up, and traded silly stories.

Geneva, where we landed, is a beautiful city, modern, clean, bustling with activity, snow capped mountains in the background. It's really a breathtaking place.

Jesus hailed a cab, and the driver took us to a gleaming building with an enormous glass façade, right in the center of town. Marching straight inside, Jesus pulled one of those Jedi mind tricks, and we walked right past the security desk and over to a bank of elevators. The elevator took us directly to the tenth floor, where the executive conference rooms were located. Stepping out into the lobby, we once again avoided detection by security. They all seemed mysteriously pre-occupied!

There was a large pair of double doors at the end of the hall toward which we now proceeded. Bursting inside, we beheld a spacious paneled room with an enormous oval table, at which at least twenty-five people were seated. Every head swung around in surprise when we entered.

Jesus strode over to the podium, switched on the microphone, and said, "Good morning, everyone! My associate here, (and here he indicated me!) told me the most amazing story this morning on the plane, and I'm here to check into it!

"It seems a friend of his contracted Lyme's disease, and the doctor prescribed a thirty-day regimen of antibiotics. So she, the friend, went to the pharmacy, and the druggist told her that the prescription would come to $1800.00!

"She went home, and went on line to see if she could do better, and she found a comparable drug for only $480.00, with a coupon. So she went back to the pharmacy, and the pharmacist filled the prescription. When she went to pay, the lady behind the counter said, 'Are you sure you want to use this coupon? These drugs are only $85.00!'

"Well, you can imagine how elated she was. She called her friend, who happens to be a physician's assistant, and told her all about it. The PA replied, 'Our Lyme's disease regimen is normally only $35.00!'

"Can anyone here explain this discrepancy in human language?"

I gathered that this was no campaign speech.

The CEO flew to his feet in a rage and slammed his fist on the table. "Who the devil are you?" he sputtered. "How did you get in here? I demand to see your credentials! How dare you interrupt our meeting?" His face was beet red and his eyes were bulging out of their sockets. This fellow was very intimidating.

Two men in dark suits arrived by a side door and stood near the exit. *Sicherheit!*

Jesus whipped open his briefcase, took out a sheet of paper, and handed it to the CEO. I have no idea what was on that paper, but the man's head snapped back, the color drained out of his face, and he became, shall we say, much more compliant. He sank back into his seat, and there was an awkward silence.

Then one of the men in attendance came to his rescue and said, "I believe I know the drug you are referring to. It is new on the market, and it contains extremely high quality ingredients. The price is high right now so that we can recoup our development costs."

That sounded plausible.

A woman across the table piped in, "We have hired a large number of PhDs and research scientists in the past year, and they come at a very high price."

I hadn't thought of that.

"I might add," said a youngish looking executive down the table, "that this company owns and operates a large state of the art facility. We maintain a very high standard!"

I could see this was true just by looking around.

Jesus spoke up, "I have conducted an independent audit, (he took out another piece of paper), and I see here that last year, after you had paid all your research and development costs, all your facilities expenses, all of your payroll, all of your corporate bonuses, all of your scholarships and philanthropic giving, you had a surplus of 500 million euros. This seems excessive."

After a brief pause, a sagacious looking gentleman sitting off to the left explained, "That money is earmarked for corporate expansion."

Everyone in the room knew that was a crock!

Jesus spoke again, "Ladies and gentlemen, you have worked hard and earned your success. And the drugs and medical devices you have developed have been truly beneficial. You have helped millions of people all over the globe.

"Just be careful that the vultures don't pick the flesh off your bones when the revolution comes. And please don't say you weren't warned!"

He nodded to me, and we left the way we had come. I was glad when we hit the street. I couldn't get out of there fast enough.

We had just enough time to catch a late lunch at a charming little café, then back to the airport for our flight home. I stumbled into my apartment just before midnight and crashed on the couch.

POST # 3 – PUB CRAWLING WITH JESUS CHRIST

Jesus called me one night last week, right out of the blue, and we arranged a meeting place downtown. It was a cool evening in late September. "Wear a necktie" was all he said.

So we met on the corner of First and Truman, and he escorted me down about half a block to a small but exclusive restaurant. When we entered, the maître d stiffly invited us to a small table by the bar, and then left to summon a waiter.

Jesus lost no time. He stood up, walked over to the bar, turned around, and threw out his favorite line in a clear crisp voice, "I'd like to buy drinks for everyone here tonight!"

There was an instant turning of heads, and expressions of surprise and disbelief, and quite frankly, annoyance.

I had to admit, he seemed completely out of place, and absurdly ridiculous.

No one took him up on his offer, or paid the least attention to him. They turned and resumed their private conversations.

Presently an obsequious little man came to our table and

said, "Mr. Korovin would like to have a word with you. Follow me."

He took us to a dark corner of the room where a savage looking young man was sitting in a plush booth, picking his teeth with a toothpick. I couldn't be sure, but I was pretty certain this fellow was the same notorious Korovin who was frequently in the papers in connection with criminal activity, and most recently with human trafficking. I was not anxious to make his acquaintance.

Mr. Korovin looked up at us and introduced himself, "My name is Korovin, and I own this establishment. Nobody buys drinks for anyone around here unless I give the go-ahead. And I don't remember giving the go-ahead!" And here he sneered, revealing his long eyeteeth and a nasty scar near his chin.

Jesus said, "I was under the impression that Boris Matvey owned this restaurant and bar."

"But I own Boris Matvey!"

Jesus slid into the booth and said, "I wonder if I might have a word with you about your business model?"

"Did I ask you to sit down?" said Korovin rudely.

"I think I could offer some suggestions that would greatly benefit your whole operation," said Jesus.

Korovin replied, "I have a better idea. How about I count to ten, and before I reach eight, you are crossing the street and losing yourself somewhere in the city. I don't care where. And take your bug-eyed assistant with you, before I sic the dogs on him!"

Bug eyed assistant? Could he possibly have been referring to me?

Jesus sat there peacefully for several minutes, until Mr. Korovin rasped, "I could have a couple of my boys help you out, if you're having trouble finding your way. I am very tired of your face right now!"

So Jesus stood up, I thought with great dignity, considering the treatment he was receiving. He walked calmly to the door, with me close beside, just to be sure that he was, ah, safe. At the door he paused for a split second, turned around, and said, "Couldn't we just chat for a few minutes?"

Mr. Korovin sprang to his feet, pointed his toothpick at us like a poison dart, and screamed, "Don't let me ever see your face again!"

So we walked out into the night.

I decided that we should go someplace for a nice cup of coffee and a donut, a little comfort food. I was just about to suggest this when we turned the corner and saw a huge flashing neon sign that proclaimed, "Go Go Nightly!"

"Oh God," I thought. "Not here. Not now."

But Jesus didn't even slow down. He marched right in the door!

Now evidently a report had spread around that a religious fanatic was on the loose, a man who called himself Jesus

Christ, and a lot of people were speculating on what this fellow's game might be.

So as soon as we entered, there was instant recognition. The girls on stage frantically grabbed any scrap of clothing they could find and went dashing off to the dressing room. The patrons, (they were all male), suddenly found they had to use the men's room, or dive under the table to retrieve a pen, or slink off to a dark corner. I recognized the mayor, and the police chief, and the president of a large bank, and the district attorney, along with numerous other luminaries from the city. Must have been boy's night out! And they were not happy to see us!

Jesus made his big announcement: "Drinks for everyone! I'm buying!"

This did very little to improve their mood. Jesus went off to find the owner, and I slinked off to a dark corner of my own.

I could hear the grumblings of the men, "What's this guy up to? I went to church already once this week! Now that Mr. Kill Joy is here, I suppose we will all have to be '*born again!*'" Etc., etc.

After about a half hour, the owner himself came out. He summoned his whole staff, the waiters, the bar tenders, the bus boys, and all the dancers. Right there in the center of his establishment he made an announcement, "I've been thinking about this for quite some time, and I've finally made up my mind. I've decided to get out of this business. I'm pretty sure I can sell this place and come out ahead, and I may try my hand at something completely different, maybe writing. I don't know. In any event, I'm sorry to break it to you this way. You've been great employees, and I know you need the work, but that's the way it is."

The stunned silence didn't last long. One of the girls said, "I'm not really surprised. I've seen it coming for a while. I actually went down to that new four-star restaurant in Chelsea, and they said they could use me. In fact it's better hours and more pay. And they said they are in need of a lot of help!"

Jesus, who had followed the owner out, now observed, "Your good looks probably won't do you any harm in that business!"

All of the girls, and the rest of the staff, decided that they were going to storm that place in the morning and grab those jobs.

This seemed to call for a celebration, and since Jesus had already offered to pay for drinks, everyone got what they wanted, and the owner supplied bar food, on the house. The patrons were not particularly pleased with the evening's developments, but they bravely joined in the festivities. They were actually surprised to discover that Jesus wasn't there to preach at them, or to moralize, or to rebuke them or correct them. They *had* been caught, after all, in a compromising situation.

But Jesus met them at their exact intellectual level. One of them, the district attorney, decided to probe him regarding a thorny issue that had plagued the city for years. Jesus' simple answer was so patently brilliant that they all sat back in utter astonishment. A kind of corporate epiphany descended on them all, and they began, right then and there, to lay plans for a complete re-organization of the city's governmental structure. If implemented, according to the mayor, it would constitute a genuine *rebirth* of the entire city going forward!

That was *his* word, not mine.

Jesus quietly moved over to where the dancers and the other employees were sitting around, making their own plans for the future. I was learning that he was an absolute master at fitting neatly into a conversation and putting everyone instantly at ease. He got them all to tell their stories, and he drew an enormous amount of humor out of them.

The girls had a brilliance all their own. I wouldn't have called them "exquisite" by any means. They possessed a rare combination of hardness and brokenness, and determination and raw courage, which, combined with their better-than-average natural good looks, made them appear almost as goddesses. Most of them, as I had suspected, turned out to be single moms, just working to keep an apartment and food on the table. They all had ambitious and noble plans for the future.

But God! They were good looking! One of them, a girl named Bonnie, was just the most gorgeous creature I had ever set eyes upon. I couldn't stop looking at her! She shot me a glance, and the chicken wing I was eating missed my mouth, smearing buffalo sauce all over my chin!

Jesus stifled a laugh, and quipped, "Easy does it there, Tiger!"

But it was too late. I was hopelessly smitten. I began to experience temporary aphasia. I could hear ringing in my ears, which grew progressively louder!

Jesus answered his cell phone, and quite abruptly he announced that we had to be going. He was already putting on his jacket and walking toward the door. I took one last look at that heavenly vision of a girl, and dashed out after him, wondering what was the almighty hurry!

He hailed a passing cab, and dropped me back at my apartment. Then he went driving off into the night.

The next morning I read in the paper that Mr. Korovin had been gunned down in the street and had died at the hospital during the night.

POST # 4 – KHARTOUM, SUDAN

"Pack a light bag. We're going to the Sudan for a few days."

So I threw one change of clothing and my shaving kit into an old knapsack, and sat on the curb outside my apartment waiting for his cab.

"Where exactly is the Sudan, anyways?" I asked him.

"Northeast Africa, just south of Egypt."

We flew all night and most of the next day, and landed in Khartoum late in the afternoon. A large black church van was there at the airport waiting for us. It turns out that Jesus had booked us into their church's schedule as a visiting preacher, and me, his assistant.

The Pastor of the church had no idea who Jesus really was. But he was excited to welcome us into his small congregation, and was looking forward to hearing Jesus' message to his flock.

When we arrived at the modest little church, the whole staff was on hand to meet us: the secretary, the housekeeper, two deacons, five religious sisters, and three young men who lived on the church property. They invited us in warmly and served us a light meal, after which we were led to our quarters to freshen up and rest.

At 7 pm that evening the whole congregation showed up, and they got right into a spirited worship service that really blew my mind. Loud, boisterous, joyful, …and something else that I couldn't quite nail down.

Then Jesus stood up and spoke for about twenty minutes in their language. His theme, I found out, was from the Old Testament "Song of Songs".

More worship and singing, after which the Pastor gave a final blessing and everyone filed out to the parking lot.

The parking area now contained four large black church vans. We began loading the vans with groceries that the people had been collecting all week, and we put as much as we could in the baggage area behind the third seat of each van.

Then everyone said goodnight, and we went to bed.

Early the next morning after a simple breakfast, we climbed into those vans with seventeen volunteers in addition to the Pastor, Jesus, and myself. There were twenty people total. Our destination was one of four camps set up for internally displaced persons in the vicinity of Khartoum, populated by people who had fled political unrest and civil war within the Sudan.

We came over a rise and into a broad, flat valley, and there, stretched out before us, was an immense sea of dirty tents, plastic sheeting, crumbling wood and brick shacks, and muddy, rutted tracks. The sun was just coming up, and so was the ever- present cloud of dust, despite the recent rain. People were beginning to emerge from wherever they slept, and campfires were beginning to pop up here and there.

We drove past the checkpoint and directly into the center of the camp, where we parked and disembarked. Several of the young men set up a crude battery-powered speaker system, whereupon Jesus, as the visiting preacher, was once again asked to deliver a short message, a small sermon. His text this time was "Come to me, all you who labor and are heavy burdened, and I will give you rest." From the response of his few listeners I gathered it was a good speech, nothing exceptional, but well received.

Then the church volunteers started handing out the food. People came with empty pots and containers and plastic bags, and the volunteers did their best to provide a small variety of food to each individual.

Jesus motioned for me to follow him, so we walked a short distance down the main track. He ducked into an old canvas tent that was indistinguishable from every other old canvas tent in the camp. I followed him inside, and when my eyes adjusted to the dark, I beheld three young Sudanese women sitting cross-legged on the dirt floor, and next to each was a young child. All three children were severely handicapped and completely disfigured. Their arms and legs were bent at grotesque angles, and their gaunt faces contained vacant eyes that rolled around in their sockets. It was the absolute picture of desolation and hopelessness.

Seeing my embarrassment and awkwardness, Jesus said,

"What you need to do is touch each one of these children." So I got down on my hands and knees and crawled around in the dirt, touching each child in turn. When I came to the last child, his mother looked at me kindly and said something I didn't understand. Jesus translated, "She would like to know how you are doing."

How was I doing? How was I doing? Could it really be that this woman, who had lost home and family and all earthly hope, could she really be asking how *I* was doing?

I tried to formulate a response for her, but a wave, a tsunami, of emotion engulfed me. I fell into her arms sobbing while she quietly consoled me.

This whole episode, to tell the truth, was completely dream-like. I felt as though I had been transported "in the spirit" to some distant place in some other universe, an almost out-of-body experience.

When we finally emerged from the tent into the full morning sun, we found the church volunteers still handing out food. I took up a station by one of the vans and started assembling food packages.

The people kept coming, and we kept distributing food as the day wore on. More and more people came, standing docilely in line, filing past our stations, picking up a supply of food for their families. At one point I looked up and saw a man walking away with a large sack of rice over his shoulder. His small son was dragging several bags of oranges wrapped in a dirty pillowcase.

And still they came, bringing their empty containers. The

volunteers cheerfully filled their sacks and baskets, and at about five o'clock in the evening the line finally dwindled, and we divided up what was left among the few remaining camp people.

The pastor said a few words of thanks to us as we packed up the sound system and prepared to return to the church.

I found Jesus standing on a rise about a hundred yards from our van. Coming up behind him, I could hear him talking, although no one else appeared to be there. He was clearly speaking words of love, evidently to some secret admirer, "These snow-capped mountains are for you! The mountain streams are yours! All the wildflowers in the valley are for you! I give them to you! I will come back for you, I promise, and take you from this squalor and filth! I promise I will come back and take you home with me!"

I searched the nearby tents to see if I could catch a glimpse of some almond-eyed beauty peering out, but I couldn't see anyone. Just the smoke of cooking fires wafting across the camp in the setting sun.

I don't know who I thought I was, but I decided I should help him focus. I asked him, "Are you running a campaign here, or a courtship?"

He turned and looked at me with the face of a grief-stricken lover and said, "Her heart beats for me alone."

I had the good sense to drop the topic!

On the way back to the church I sat next to a young man, William, who spoke excellent English. I said, "Is it just me, or did we hand out an enormous quantity of food today?"

He replied, "Its been happening for about a year now. Every week we collect whatever food we can spare, and on Saturday we come out here and pass it out. God only knows how many people are being fed."

So I started doing some figuring. Twenty volunteers handing out food for nine straight hours. Each volunteer spent about one minute with each person from the camp, or sixty people per hour. And each camp dweller left with enough food for a family of four, on average. That comes to a staggering 40,000 people fed from those four church vans, and this a weekly occurrence!

I wanted to shout that we had just witnessed the greatest miracle ever recorded in human history, but the other volunteers were fast asleep by now, and Jesus was in the front seat chatting with the pastor, in an effort to keep him from dozing at the wheel.

I fell into my old habit of daydreaming. I thought of the gospel where Jesus fed the multitudes. There were 5000 men at that time, maybe 20,000 total if you counted women and children. Here today we had twice that many.

There, Jesus had twelve helpers. Here we had twenty.

There, Jesus had five loaves and two fish. Here we had four van loads.

There, the people ate and were satisfied. Here, there was barely enough to stay alive.

There, twelve baskets of leftovers were collected. I doubt

there were any leftovers here.

There, the people realized what Jesus had done, and wanted to make him king. Here, the people showed up every Saturday for another food program administered by those nice church workers.

I also wondered if the novelty of the miracle had worn off long ago, and now the small church congregation was being stretched to the limit, close to exhaustion, caring for the basic needs of a forgotten and discarded segment of humanity.

And this was just one of four camps in the vicinity of Khartoum.

In the Sudan itself, or just over the border in Chad, there are well over five million souls living in the confines of semi-permanent tent cities, without any realistic hope of ever returning to their former lives. I wondered who was taking care of them?

Those were a few days that will be forever etched in my memory.

POST # 5 – PUB CRAWLING WITH JESUS CHRIST

"Interested in going out for a drink?"

It was Jesus. Normally I would jump at the chance to be with him. But lately I had discovered that going to a bar with him meant putting my own life at risk. I hesitantly accepted.

"Great! How about we meet at the sixth street bus station in half an hour?"

I met him there, and we strolled down the block. He looked sharp this evening. His slacks were neatly pressed and his beard was neatly trimmed, and he looked excited to be going out!

"Mind if I ask where we are going?"

"I thought we'd try a bar up on Jackson Street."

The bar had no identifying signs or indicators, no special labels, but as soon as we entered there was no doubt whatsoever what kind of bar it was. I thought, "Well, this should be educational."

Jesus made his opening gambit. Moving right to the bar, he gazed over the crowd, then announced in a loud but friendly voice that he would like to buy everyone a drink.

There was the normal surprise at this announcement. But all conversation ceased and was replaced by a long stony silence.

I clearly detected an undercurrent of mild hostility.

A man down the bar broke the silence: "We don't actually *need* someone to buy our drinks. We feel perfectly capable of purchasing and consuming our own refreshments, thank you very much!"

Then a fleeting thought crossed his mind. "Hey, you're that odd religious fellow that's been seen around, calling yourself 'Jesus Christ', and running for President of the World! Whatever your game is, we're not having any! We've heard your hokey stories about 'mercy'. Not impressed!"

Somebody yelled out, "How about showing some mercy toward us?"

Jesus turned around and asked the bartender for two glasses of water. We sat down at a table near the center of the room. Taking a sip of his water, Jesus replied, "What kind of mercy are you looking for?"

That did the trick. One, then another, then another of these men spat out in harsh tones the most incredible stories of ridicule, abuse, hostility, prejudice, and rejection imaginable. Jesus listened attentively and never once interrupted.

Then he threw out the bait: "I happen to run an organization that would certainly be able to offer help."

A serious looking young man stepped forward. "I presume you are referring to *the church!* If so, that is the last place on earth that any of us would ever turn to for help! A God-awful collection of hypocrites and perverts if ever there was one!"

Jesus smiled and asked, "With whom do I have the pleasure of speaking?"

"George Atwood" was the curt reply.

"Well, George Atwood, tell me something. Have you ever built an organization up from nothing, seen it flourish, and felt proud of your accomplishment?"

"As a matter of fact, I have." said Mr. Atwood. "I began the very first chapter of the LGBT advocacy group at the state university ten years ago, and it has grown to be a powerful voice in our state government to this very day. Yes, I am extremely proud of my accomplishment!"

"Well then you and I understand each other perfectly!" said Jesus.

"You may be proud of your church, but you people have carefully and shamefully excluded all of us here," said George Atwood. "Your homophobic friend there, the one they mistakenly refer to as *Saint* Paul, was very careful to single us out as *undesirable.*"

"I see what you mean," said Jesus, "But you could hardly say he was *singling* you out. He also mentioned murderers, adulterers, gossips, slanderers, people like that!"

"Is this supposed to make me feel better?" asked Atwood.

Jesus responded, "Saint Paul forgot to mention that other group of undesirables: Carpenters, electricians, and plumbers! If they think they're getting into my organization they have another thing coming!"

What? *"Where are we going with this?"* I thought.

George Atwood stared straight ahead. His face was a mixture of disappointment and growing anger. He said, "I thought we were having an intelligent conversation, but I can see now that you are simply here to ridicule us, like a lot of your kind. So good evening to you, sir!"

With that he spun around and stormed away.

Jesus said nothing. He arched his eyebrow at me. He took a sip of water. He tapped his fingers lightly on the table.

After about five minutes George Atwood returned. "Okay, what's the joke? I'm dying to hear the punch line! Who, then, gets into your organization?"

Jesus said, "George, please sit down and let me buy you a drink. I'm not trying to bribe you or gain power over you. It's just a friendly gesture. You can buy the next round, if you like. And I'd like to buy a round for your friends, if you don't mind."

So George agreed, and the tension eased considerably.

"You had a question?" asked Jesus.

"Yes. Who… or should I say, *how*, does someone get into your *organization*, as you call it?"

"An excellent question! And here's the answer. First, you must read my campaign literature. Second, you must cast your vote *in my favor!* Then, and only then, will I invite you to join my organization.

"Furthermore, it is just an *invitation.* You would not be required to join if you didn't want. But nobody gets in without going directly through *me.* That's how I stay on top of things."

George thought about this. "Let me get this straight. Are you saying that all those people that Paul excluded can get in just by voting for you?"

"That is correct. Paul, of course, was a murderer himself!"

There was a noticeable shifting of furniture in the room.

"Hypothetically", said Atwood, "Hypothetically, if I were to read your literature, say, and vote for you, but declined your invitation, what then? Where would that leave us?"

"I would be eternally grateful to you for casting a vote in my favor. I would never forget you. And when I successfully accomplish my political goal, you would find yourself in a very favorable position."

"I see." said Atwood. "I will definitely have to think about that. So, then (not that I would ever be interested) suppose someone were to *accept* your invitation. What then?"

"Well then," said Jesus, "I would put you in a six month training program, we would make some agreements, there would be some initiation ceremonies, and you would be in! Simple!"

George mused, "Two things I could never see myself doing: Raising my hands and shouting 'Praise the Lord!', and subjecting myself to that pointless and ridiculous baptismal nonsense!"

"Save your praise for after the election!" said Jesus. "But I absolutely *insist* on the Baptism. And after that ceremonial bath, I will go in with a pick and a shovel and a contractor's bag, and clear out thirty years worth of sludge and filth and smut. I will scrape your insides until you shine like a new pair of combat boots!"

Here Jesus stood up and spoke to the whole crowd, "I don't care what anyone looks like. I believe in cleaning the *inside* of the cup!

"I am not here to trifle with you! I could definitely use your vote. But what I am really interested in is recruiting some young men and women for my currently developing rapid deployment squad. I need people who are willing to jump out of an airplane if I say we need to jump! I am looking for individuals who are fearless in the face of ridicule, abuse, prejudice, rejection.

"Would you think about this? Would you give it some consideration? In view of your life up to this point, what have you got to lose?"

Now this was something new to these men. Here was a powerful and attractive man standing in front of them, directly challenging them to a future that was at once exciting and at the same time terrifying, on many levels. There were no guarantees, no safety nets, no fall back positions. About the only attractive thing about it was the dynamic presence of Jesus himself!

The room returned to silence. But it wasn't the stony silence of before. It was a thoughtful silence. These men were thinking hard.

And I would like to think that some of them were right on the verge of stepping forward.

But what might have happened is not important. What did happen is what counts. What did happen utterly destroyed the moment. The mood was smashed, completely, like a shattered glass of champagne.

Out of the shadows stepped a very tall man, dressed completely in drag, with long dirty yellow hair and teeth and fingernails. Bright red lipstick was smeared around his mouth. He came strutting forward and said in a high falsetto voice, "I'd just love to join up with your organization. That sounds simply divine!" He leered over at me and said, "Where do I sign, sweetheart?" He had a large feathered boa wrapped around his neck, and his fishnet stockings clearly revealed a "boa" of a different sort!

Jesus took one look at him and spoke directly to the snake: "Get out of him, and stop bothering him!"

The tall transvestite stopped in her tracks. Tears welled up in her eyes, her lips formed a pout, and she stamped her foot on the floor like a little girl. She looked like she was going to burst into tears. She tried to take another step forward, but whatever muscular-skeletal system was holding her up failed at that exact moment, and she collapsed to the floor in a perfect face plant, breaking her nose in the process.

Someone ran to the bar and got a bucket of ice water, which he dumped right on her head.

She came to, and pulled herself back up by grabbing the back of a chair. She was a mess, with blood and water and lipstick all over the place, and now she was crying in earnest. I mean she was bawling, really wailing! Come to think of it, she was shrieking like a banshee from a late night horror flick.

Jesus' steady gaze was unflinching. He repeated his command, "Get out of him! Leave him alone!"

This time it looked like someone smacked this creature right on the forehead with a two by four. She went careening backwards and landed with a thud on her back, bouncing once on the bar room floor.

Another ice water bath brought the man to his senses, and he sat up and looked around with clear eyes. Someone helped him to his feet, and he sat down at our table, looking rather disoriented. Incredulously, he said, "This may be hard to believe, but I heard every word you said before, and I really do want to join with you. I know I'm not much of a candidate, but I am prepared to do whatever it takes!"

But Jesus strongly advised against it. He said, "I think you should go home, reconnect with your family, and pick up your life where you left off fifteen years ago."

Recollection and determination crept into the man's face. He rose to his feet, put on a borrowed trench coat, and walked out the door.

Jesus turned to the room and said, "There will be blood, and there will be screaming!"

The manager of the bar came over and asked us in no uncertain terms to please leave the premises immediately, and not to plan on returning.

POST # 6 – PARIS/HAITI

"I need you to accompany me for a short stay in Paris. Pack lightly, we may be on the move!"

I made arrangements with my office, and soon we were arriving in Paris, where we booked into a fine boutique hotel in the heart of the Parisian Left Bank.

Ah Paris! Je t'aime!

We dressed casually, (the only kind of clothes I packed!), and went out the first evening, heading down a few narrow streets toward the Seine. A few more twists and turns took us to a place called "The Batcave", or "La Batcave" in French. We got past the bouncer, went through a few doors, and emerged into a gigantic and cavernous bomb shelter to the sound of ear-splitting industrial trance music and pulsating swirling multicolored lights and torches, where hundreds of young bodies were swaying and bumping to the beat. The people looked absolutely death-like with the black clothing and body piercings. I was certain that every Goth in Paris was right here in this place.

Jesus went straight for the sound booth. I loved it when he did this. Somehow he marched in, flicked off the music, flicked on the house lights, and said in a pleasant voice, "I'd like to invite everyone here to a party tomorrow afternoon at 2:00 pm, (and here he mentioned an address in the wealthy Maisons-Laffitte suburb of Paris). He repeated the time and address, said "See you there tomorrow!" and with a friendly wave of his hand he flicked off the house lights, flicked on the music, and marched right back out, before anyone could even process what had just taken place. He came over to me and said, "Let's get out of here!"

So we ducked back out into the alley, and before too long we arrived at a grand hotel right off the Champs Elysees. On the way, I inquired about this party that he had mentioned.

"Yes, I've got to get busy with those arrangements!"

We entered the hotel and we were immediately escorted into a grand dining room, heavy with crystal chandeliers and golden statues. I said, (to myself), "Now this is what *I'm* talking about!"

Obviously, I never knew quite what to expect next.

Soon after we were seated, Jesus excused himself for a minute, walked over to a nearby table, and struck up a conversation with an aristocratic looking gentleman and his diamond-studded wife. Taking a seat at their table, he chatted amiably with them and seemed to reach some kind of an agreement. Soon enough they shook hands, and Jesus returned to our table.

"Looks like we're all set for tomorrow's party!" he said.

Now, I probably don't need to mention that wherever he went, Jesus raised considerable interest just by the force of his presence and persona. He was a people magnet. He went to no special trouble to conceal his identity, although preferring to engage people on their own terms, something he did in a most natural and graceful manner. Even still, he was a sensation wherever we went. Heads would turn when we walked by, and I am certain they weren't looking at me!

But tonight I witnessed a phenomenon that was unlike any of our previous soirees.

There was a bit of whispered conversation in the room. Then, one by one, the most dignified and extravagantly dressed couples began coming to our table to…well, it was unmistakable! They were coming to pay him homage! I don't know who these people were, but they could easily have been the royalty of Europe. The huge room became quietly electric. The waiters paused. The entire kitchen staff silently filed out to have a look. All of the hotel employees soundlessly appeared.

Jesus rose to his feet. He was a middle-aged man, plainly dressed, with well-proportioned features and broad shoulders. He stood in the center of the room without a podium or microphone. His simple, modest, almost austere, presence was more majestic than all the riches of Paris.

He spoke easily and freely in French, "My friends, our time is quickly approaching. All of you have devoted yourselves to me for years, and now the tide is beginning to turn in our favor! I have you to thank! I love you all! Your dedication has meant everything to me! I'm asking you to continue exerting your influence on my behalf and to remain vigilante. In a very short while you will taste victory with me. I'm looking forward with great anticipation to the time when I can properly thank you!"

Then he sat down, and while I tried to make some headway on my coq au vin, a continuous stream of people came and passed by our table to shake his hand and wish him well. Many of them were weeping openly. He introduced me to every one of them, as if I were a person of importance!

Finally he said to all of them, "My friend and I have got to be going. We have a big day tomorrow. Your kindness to me tonight is deeply appreciated. You have my blessing. You can be sure of that!"

And with that, we departed.

The following day at about 1:00 pm a Rolls Royce Limousine pulled up in front of our hotel, and we were driven to a palatial mansion in the northwestern section of Paris. The house was a huge stone edifice with a mansard roof, set back on a gracefully sloping lawn, with a long circular drive leading right to the front door. The interior of the house was lavish, opulent, and stunning. Servants were busily making preparations, setting out chairs and tables, bringing large trays of food from the kitchen. A string quartet was tuning up in the corner, flowers were being arranged, and it looked for all the world like a wedding reception.

At just about 2:15, the visitors began arriving, roaring up the driveway in their high-performance European roadsters, in groups of two or three per car. Tossing the keys to a valet, they strode right in without a moment's hesitation, never even slowing down to admire the fine boxwood hedges. Despite their frightful appearance and bored expression, they were not without social confidence. They were all from old and wealthy families, and they were perfectly at home in this stately mansion. About 140 guests showed up, which I thought was just remarkable. I doubted anyone at all would come.

The affair was beginning to look like something out of "The Great Gatsby", or "The Count of Monte Cristo", but unlike those stories, Jesus was not at all aloof or calculating. He plowed right into the middle of his guests and began at once to break down their resistance by talking about art and music and fashion and the kind of current events that interested them. He quickly got their names and their pulse, and his jokes were so ridiculous that they laughed in spite of themselves. The food was luscious, the young people were among friends, and the afternoon turned out to be a great success. Jesus somehow got them all out on the spacious back lawn and organized an impromptu soccer tournament, a sport that these rich kids were passionate about and were quite good at, having been educated at some of the very best European boarding schools.

After the tournament, and after a colossal Venetian desert table was rolled out, Jesus stood up and casually mentioned that he was running a mission trip to Haiti, a building project, and would anyone care to join him the following week? A small donation of €1000 would be required to help defray the cost of travel and building materials.

The money was no object, and the idea seemed almost pleasantly diverting, considering the normal boredom that faced them. Thirty-five young men and women signed on for the trip.

I suppose I should have stopped my post here, and started another to cover the Haiti trip, but the two events were so closely related that I decided to report them as one continuous episode. Besides, the Haiti trip consisted mostly of mixing concrete and playing soccer.

The interim week in and around Paris was as fine a time as I have ever spent.

Jesus and I met all thirty-five volunteers at the airport the following week. The black clothing had miraculously turned to khaki, and the bored expressions had mitigated considerably. We flew non-stop to Port–au-Prince and were met once again by the ubiquitous black church vans, which took us to a remote spot on the far outskirts of the city. Grinding poverty and burning garbage were everywhere, but we arrived at a mission outpost that was surprisingly clean and orderly. We met the four deacons who were to be our guides and construction foremen, and after getting situated in barrack-style dorms, we got a tour of the project that was underway.

Sixty-five concrete and block houses were in the very early stages of construction. The work that was assigned to us was simple, straightforward, and labor intensive, not anything a person would care to make a career of, in my judgment.

The following day we got started early. The deacons split

us up into four teams of nine, five girls and four guys to a team. The girls mixed concrete and fetched water, while the guys carried the concrete to the forms, and the deacon foreman did the rodding and finishing. Jesus turned the whole thing into a sporting event, pitting one team against the next, and in no time the construction, and the competition, advanced at a furious rate. The winning team got the first showers at the end of the day, so things got pretty intense as the day wore on. Following dinner, the competition resumed as the four teams battled it out on the soccer field.

Each day, one of the deacons would take his team into the city to expose them to the reality that was Haiti. Our team ended up going to a large clinic that was almost exclusively dedicated to the care of abandoned infants, run by the Missionary Sisters of the Poor, a group of nuns who were completely overwhelmed by the enormity of the task. Our small group was ushered into the nursery to have a look.

One of the girls expressed surprise that a nursery would be so uncharacteristically quiet. In fact, the place was eerily silent. The nun in charge explained, "We do what we can. We have barely enough time to see that the children are fed and changed. But they never get held or fondled. They are starved for a mother's touch. Some barely survive a month, despite the fact that they get adequate nourishment."

These formerly dead punk rockers snapped in that moment. The girls each went like magnets to a dirty bassinet and gently picked up one of those helpless little babies, rocking them tenderly in their arms, smiling through a torrent of tears. The guys just stood there trying desperately to keep from breaking down. I found myself, once again, crying uncontrollably.

The ride back to the mission was completely silent.

We finished out the week having pushed the construction project forward considerably, and on the last day, coming back to the mission, we came upon a long row of tables set up outside on the hillside, with white tablecloths and wild flowers in small vases. The tables were set for a festive dinner, with clear plastic glasses and good quality paper plates, and all the families that were destined to occupy our small concrete houses were there to serve us a farewell meal. Candles were lit, and just as the sun was setting, Jesus stood up to offer a blessing. He took a large loaf of bread, and dividing it up, he passed it down the table. Then he took sips from two glasses of local wine, and passed the glasses down the table as well.

It occurred to me that this was the first time I ever actually observed an alcoholic beverage pass his lips, despite the numerous evenings we spent in bars and fine restaurants.

As we sipped more wine and ate from the small platters of cheese and olives on the table, Jesus gave a short reflection on the surpassing value of human labor.

Then everyone pitched in and served the dinner. All the families joined us around the table, and we sat there feasting until the sky was pitch black and multitudes of brilliant stars seemed within easy reach of our hands.

The beauty of those hours was simply beyond description.

Each one of the young French volunteers turned out to be a gem, richly gifted with wit, intelligence, sympathy, and a desire to do the right thing. All they needed was a leader.

And isn't that what this is all about, after all?

I could barely stand to part with these wonderful new friends.

POST # 7 – LIMA, PERU

"Tonight, I thought we'd go to Lima, Peru! No luggage required."

I was going to have to get used to this kind of travel!

We got on a flight at around midnight, and early the next morning we landed in Lima. We got transportation into the center of the city, and made our way immediately to the ancient and very humble shrine of Saint Rose. A Catholic mass was in progress, so we stayed until it's conclusion, then we casually walked around the grounds. Jesus was in deep thought. We came to a fairly modern looking stone statue of a young and fragile Saint Rose, gazing up into heaven. Jesus must have stood staring at her for twenty minutes.

Now, Saint Rose is absolutely adored by the people of Lima. She is the patron of all of Peru. They are fascinated by her. She was extremely penitential and mystical when she was alive. She was also reported to have been ravishingly beautiful. Jesus was transfixed.

Following that interlude, we made our way to the Plaza Major, the central square of the city. The so called "Changing of the Guard" was just getting underway directly in front of the presidential palace, so we took seats on the bleachers that had been erected for just that purpose. The changing of the guard is a ceremony that takes place entirely on horseback, an equestrian extravaganza, with fine looking men in handsome military uniforms riding on splendid steeds adorned and festooned with all sorts of ribbons and banners. They rode around and around in intricate patterns, brandishing their swords and following the shouted commands of their officers. There was an entire military band, also on horseback, playing continuous marching music. It was a spectacular display.

At one point, I "came to" and realized that they were playing none other than Verdi's Triumphal March, from Aida! I thought to myself, "Why, they could be practicing for Jesus' big inaugural day, for all I know!"

As if in answer to my thoughts, Jesus leaned over and said, "If the leaders of the world wanted to meet with me in Lima, Peru, I wouldn't object."

I didn't have much time to think about that, because the ceremony was over, and we were headed over to the national cathedral, a very old and complicated building which also faces the main square.

To help us navigate the cathedral, we joined a large tour group just getting underway. The tour was being led by a woman named Lilly, a woman who thoroughly enjoyed her job. She had more information stored in her brain than anyone could possibly absorb in a lifetime, and it flowed out of her mouth in happy torrents. Jesus was delighted with her. To tease her he kept asking inane questions like, "Are you sure that's baroque, and not rococo?" She just laughed, and to punish him she ramped up the flow of details and descriptions until we were practically buried under an avalanche of information. When we finally stumbled out of there my head was swimming and I needed a cup of the matte d cocoa to soothe my jangled nerves.

I was beginning to discover that Jesus was a high-energy type of person, and Jesus on holiday was like the mayor of a city on steroids. If he had been alone I'm sure he would have knocked on every door of every house, every church, every office, and every building in the entire city. He would have gone in, sat down, had tea, met the people, and learned their life story. For my sake he limited himself to a few government buildings, a few shops, and about forty spontaneous interviews with complete strangers on the street. They were charmed with him, and he was totally absorbed with them. I got the impression that if they had known who he really was, they would have treated him exactly the same! Lima was a city he loved!

Would this be a good city for an inaugural celebration? I decided that it couldn't be more perfect. The air quality is not great, and the traffic is a nightmare, but these are issues that could be resolved. Lima has a fine international airport right within the confines of the city. The city itself, overlooking the Pacific Ocean, is situated in the center of Peru, which is itself situated in the center of South America, on the west coast. Half of the major countries in South America border Peru in a crescent fashion beginning with Ecuador to the north, followed in clockwise direction by Columbia, Brazil, Bolivia, and Chile to the south.

The government leaves it's citizens alone. Internationally, Peru is not a political "hot spot". They are able to get along with other people. Their major international dispute seems to be with Chile, and the issue is, which country, exactly, is responsible for the development of *pisco,* their high proof grape brandy.

Lima sits high on a cliff overlooking the Pacific Ocean, affording spectacular views, and a perfect launching pad for the very popular hang gliders. Their beaches are a surfer's paradise. The city is currently constructing a beautiful walking esplanade that stretches for miles along the shore, and if this weren't enough, Peru now boasts of world-class cuisine, perhaps best exemplified by the renowned *ceviche.*

We finished the day by dining on this exact dish at a five star restaurant in the heart of beautiful Miraflores. Then it was off to the airport for another overnight flight back home.

I arrived at my office a little late that next day.

POST # 8 – GREAT NEWS!

I got an embossed invitation in the mail, requesting the honor of my presence at an evening reception to be held at the downtown Hilton, one day last week. It was of course from Jesus.

I actually put on a black suit for the occasion, and bought a new necktie just to show that I was still "in the game", so to speak.

The invitation said seven o'clock, but when I arrived at six-fifty, the room was already full. I'll bet there were seventy people there. At first I thought we were all perfect strangers, but as I looked around, I began to see some familiar faces. Across the room I noticed the young executive from Geneva. When he saw me he tossed me a smile and a wave. Then I noticed William from the Sudan, and Lilly, the laughing lady from Lima. Even Jerry Donovan was there. Over on one side I saw the ever thoughtful and serious George Atwood. Quite a shock to see him! When he saw me, however, he smiled and gave me a "thumbs up", and mouthed the words, "Praise the Lord!"

There were tables set up in the center of the room with lovely French pastries, cheese, and fruit. I discovered the affair was being catered by one of my new Parisian friends,

Jacques. Platters of fresh oysters and chilled French wine in fluted glasses were a featured item.

At exactly seven, Jesus stood up at the podium and began the evening by thanking us all for being there. "Great news!" he said. "I have hired an independent polling company, and the results are just astonishing. I know there is a margin of error, and the results may be skewed in my favor, but for the first time *ever*, my numbers are up to nearly fifty percent. The poll was a broad sweeping affair, combining both hard votes and approval ratings, but we are definitely trending up, and the indications are beyond dispute!

"I invited you here tonight because it is directly due to you and your recent efforts on my behalf that we have come this far. Your hard work has really paid off! We are on the move, and nothing can slow us down as long as you are on my team! I am absolutely thrilled with this latest development, and I wanted to be here with you all to celebrate!"

He gushed for a few more minutes, then jumped down from the dais and made his way into our midst.

I got into a conversation with some of the other attendees, who evidently had been traveling around with Jesus much the same as I had. We came to the conclusion among ourselves that if we took all of our accomplishments and put them into a pile, it wouldn't amount to a hill of beans! But there was Jesus, extolling us to the skies, as if we were really something marvelous.

I noticed a table across the room, surrounded by a number

of people, so I went over to check it out. The table was covered with dark blue knapsacks. A well-dressed man behind the table asked my name, and then handed me a knapsack, crossed my name off his list, and said "Congratulations!"

I looked at the sturdy knapsack. It was a rich navy blue color, with a handsome white dove embroidered on the back. Under the dove was my name, and under my name was the word "apostle".

As I stood there with my mouth gaping open, I heard others nearby expressing the same sentiments of surprise and wonder. My mind was absolutely reeling at the implications. Then from behind I heard a voice say, "Hey, Tiger Man! I was hoping to see you here tonight!"

I spun around and found myself not more than two feet from my gorgeous go-go girl, Bonnie! She was holding her blue backpack in her hands. My powers of cognitive thought fled to an unavailable portion of my brain, and I think I said something like, "Hey… I was hoping to see you tonight…too!" It was really bad. But she grinned happily, and I was saved from ruining that conversation any further because just at that moment Jesus got back on the stage and said,

"I hope everyone has retrieved their backpack by now. Just a little token of my enormous appreciation. I simply cannot express my gratitude adequately. I hope you are enjoying this reception!"

There was an enormous burst of applause at this.

Jesus continued, "We have the hall for another two hours. Please have fun and get acquainted. But after that I need you to go home and pack your new blue luggage."

"I will meet you all at the airport in the morning."

Then Jesus clutched the podium, and in a trembling voice almost breathless with excitement, he said, "Tomorrow, we head to the *Middle East!*"

The End

Made in the USA
San Bernardino, CA
17 December 2015